'Annie, are you...
hell is Zach do...

Annie sighed as her b...
law—entered the roo...
coming. She'd played referee between brother and
sister more times than she could count.

'Sit down, Lucy,' Annie said. 'I've got something to
tell you.'

'All I want to know is what that bastard's doing in
your house. After what he did to you…'

Zach turned to his sister. 'What did I do to *you* to
make you hate me so much?'

'You turned your back on me when I needed a big
brother! You rejected our family to become some
hotshot in town. And you rejected Annie when you
hit the big time. Three strikes and you're out,
brother dear. Annie—'

'Stop that, Lucy.' Annie's voice was firm. 'I can
speak for myself. Besides, what happens between
Zach and me is *our* business. Now, please listen to
what I have to say.'

'Nothing you could say will make me change my
mind about him!'

'Not even if I told you you're going to be an aunt?'

Lucy's mouth gaped. 'An aunt?' Her eyes dropped
to Annie's stomach. *'An aunt?'*

Dear Reader,

Welcome to Superromance!

We have some lovely stories for you this month, starting with the third instalment of RIVERBEND, where Laura Abbot's *Homecoming* gives us a reunion story with a kick. Don't forget to look out for *Last-Minute Marriage* by Marisa Carroll next month.

Christine Rimmer brings a little glamour to the proceedings with *The Bravo Billionaire* which uncovers more Bravo family secrets. The Bravo family returns to Special Edition next month with *The Marriage Conspiracy*.

We also have *Just One Night* by Kathryn Shay, which is our 9 MONTHS LATER story, and a search for a lost love with an unexpected twist in Judith Arnold's *Found: One Wife*.

Enjoy!

The Editors

Just One Night

KATHRYN SHAY

SILHOUETTE
SUPERROMANCE

*Silhouette, Silhouette Superromance and Colophon are
registered trademarks of Harlequin Books S.A., used under licence.*

*First published in Great Britain 2002
Silhouette Books, Eton House, 18-24 Paradise Road,
Richmond, Surrey TW9 1SR*

© Mary Catherine Schaefer 1997

ISBN 0 373 70760 6

38-1002

*Printed and bound in Spain
by Litografia Rosés S.A., Barcelona*

Dear Reader,

In this book I wanted to explore the bond children bring to a relationship. While pregnant with my daughter, almost seventeen years ago, I kept a daily journal detailing my feelings about being pregnant for the first time. What it was like to give birth and how I felt afterwards—about her *and* her father. I remember clearly—as if it were yesterday—the incredible closeness I felt with my husband when we brought this little life into the world together. I have never loved him more.

I've tried to capture that feeling with Zach and Annie. I hope you enjoy their story.

Kathryn Shay

PS I love to hear from readers. You can reach me at: PO Box 24288, Rochester, New York 14624-0288, USA.

To Jerry, again.
When you read this book, you'll know why.

CHAPTER ONE

THE BUILDING that housed Sloan Associates in downtown Lansing, Massachusetts, was as intimidating and apparently as impenetrable as Zachary Sloan, its owner—and Annie Montgomery's ex-husband.

"I'm sorry, Mr. Sloan is at a meeting." The receptionist, a fortyish woman of formidable height, peered down at Annie. "And he doesn't see *anyone* without an appointment."

Oh, fine, I'll just make an appointment to give him the worst news of his life—that he's going to be a father.

Keeping the sarcastic retort to herself, Annie sighed and pushed her hair out of her eyes. The dragon lady had a right to look at her askance. Annie knew she was a mess. She'd been sick twice already and it was only ten o'clock in the morning. She'd come right from the doctor's office to Zach's, fearing that if she gave herself the time, she'd lose her nerve.

Just as her mother had done. Consequently, Annie had never known her own father. There had been tension between Sonya Montgomery and Annie for years because of it.

So now, determined not to repeat Sonya's mistake,

Annie stood bedraggled and bewildered in Zach's office, shakier than she'd ever been in her life. Meanwhile, the receptionist was eyeing her clothes—a loose calf-length navy-blue and white plaid dress with a dropped waist. She'd thrown an old white sweater over it, and slipped into the nearest shoes—a pair of well-worn sneakers. She hadn't managed any jewelry—not even a watch.

Early refugee, Zach had affectionately called the way she dressed. Annie shopped at consignment stores, and Zach had teased her about her preferences—until he'd become the rising young executive. Then his silent disapproval and subtle hints had led her to designer labels for company events and evenings out. When she left Zach, Annie had packed up all those clothes and donated them to the Salvation Army. Their opposing taste in fashion was only one of a myriad of differences between them.

As another wave of nausea hit Annie, she grabbed on to the edge of the desk.

"Are you all right?" At least the receptionist's voice held some sympathy.

Annie nodded. "I'll be leaving in a minute."

"Would you like to make an appointment to see Mr. Sloan?"

Annie shook her head. Making an appointment to tell Zach of his impending fatherhood would be humiliating. Maybe she'd try to call him at home. Or maybe she should leave a message for him to call her. Despite how she'd hurt him four weeks ago, he'd at least return her call, wouldn't he?

"Can I leave him a message?"

The woman looked doubtful.

She probably thinks I'm another one of his conquests.

You are, honey.

The thought made her sicker. She breathed deeply and tried to smile but her stomach felt as if it was on rinse cycle.

Quickly, Annie scrawled a short note to Zach, thanked the clearly bemused receptionist and headed for the elevator. But the thought of going up or down just then made her seek sanctuary in a corner of the large sitting area that faced the elevator. Exhausted, she sank onto an overstuffed couch and lay her head back on the thick cushions.

Everything about this office complex was rich and plush. Appointed in polished brass, marble and glass, it suited the man *Architectural Digest* had called "a young Frank Lloyd Wright," when Zach had designed the Pierce Museum. Built six years ago, amid critical speculation that the design was too radical, the museum had been his first real triumph. She could still see his blue eyes glimmering with pleasure at the plans. *It's the best thing I've ever done, Annie. It's going to get me everything I want.*

Which was, of course, everything Annie *didn't* want.

Following the memory came the image of Zach's

taut face four weeks ago when he strode to the perimeter of the museum—then surrounded by ambulances, fire trucks and police cars. The emergency teams were there to rescue the fifty people who'd been at a fund-raising dinner when the staircase—the building's most striking feature—had collapsed. Annie had arrived on the scene as part of the Red Cross Disaster Relief and Rescue Unit. Her heart had skidded to a halt at her first glimpse of Zach in five years...

"Annie? What are you doing here?"

"I work for the Red Cross."

"I didn't know." He held up rolled blueprints. "I was told to bring the plans. Where are the engineers?"

Annie pointed to where the city engineers, the builder, Martin Mann, and the original structural engineer, Les Corrigan, had gathered to figure out a way to shore up the staircase so the rescue could begin. Zach joined them and had spent the next couple of hours directing the efforts to install rebars— the steel reinforcing beams that would hold up the rest of the staircase.

Annie closed her eyes, trying to block out the sights and sounds of the disaster...

"We got one of them out, Annie," a fireman had shouted. "He needs the ambulance." Two firemen whisked a stretcher past her. On it a young man lay unconscious, his limbs at awkward angles, bright red blood oozing from a gash on his arm. Annie scooped up a clipboard and a walkie-talkie and said, "Unit one. Pull in. Immediate departure…"

Next came a woman. Her once-styled hair was matted with blood. Already her face had swollen black and blue and her arms hung down like a rag doll's. Her long evening gown was ripped up the side and covered with blood. Annie's stomach had lurched at the sight, but she'd immediately quelled the response and crossed to the stretcher with blankets.

Then a burly policeman and his partner wheeled out an older man. The victim's once-pristine shirt was red with blood. He was moaning. Annie wished she could shut out the sound…

All the horror of that evening had led Annie to do the stupidest thing she'd done in years. In fact, her foolish actions that night had landed her here, sick, sitting in Zach's waiting area a month later…

Zach had stayed the whole night, serving food, gathering medical supplies and even assisting with the rescue. Thirty-three people had escaped unhurt physically, although all had been traumatized by being inside the building as the staircase collapsed. Ten had minor cuts and bruises, treated at the site. Six people had been severely injured and taken to the hospital. One woman had been killed.

When the rescue operation was finally over at 4:00 a.m., Annie had considered going home with her co-workers and leaving Zach alone.

But remembering the boy she'd married when she

was nineteen, and the man she'd loved for years after that, despite their differences, she simply couldn't abandon him to his fears.

Instead, she said, "Come on, Zach. It won't help to stay. You can give me a ride home."

His bleak eyes riveted on her face. "If you're sure there's nothing else I can do."

They headed toward the cars parked along a blacktop that abutted the museum. At the perimeter of the parking lot, the media had kept vigil through the night. Like vultures, several reporters swooped down on them.

A man with a name tag that read J. Gumby shoved a microphone at Zach. "You're Zachary Sloan, aren't you?"

Lights from a camera shone in their faces. Annie raised her hand to shield her eyes; Zach did the same.

Questions came at them like rapid-fire bullets. "What did you find out about the building?... Whose fault was the collapse?... Will the gallery owners sue?... Do you think the dead woman's family will come after you?... Are you fearful of losing your business?"

Zach shouldered their way through the crowd, shaking his head silently as the reporters pelted him with questions. Deftly he maneuvered Annie and himself into his car. "Let's get out of here," he said as the engine roared to life and they sped away. About a block from the museum, he pulled over in the parking lot of an all-night convenience store. He shut off the engine and leaned back against the leather seat. His hair, the exact color and texture of fine-grain sand, was peppered with dirt, and grime still covered his cheeks. He looked exhausted and vulnerable.

"I...I hadn't thought about...it never entered my mind...about lawsuits...the legal ramifications of this."

"I'm sorry," Annie said, needing to comfort him. "Maybe you shouldn't be alone right now."

"Why?" The question lacked challenge, a fact that confirmed how overwrought he was. She herself was stricken by the death of the woman and the injuries of several other people. And Annie was a pro at this. It was all new to the man beside her who was clearly suffering.

"It's called rescuer's trauma. In any disaster-relief work, the volunteers, as well as trained personnel, are stunned and horrified like you are. Many seek therapy after what they've seen and dealt with. It's like war veterans who experience post-traumatic stress syndrome."

"What about you?"

"I've had my share of visits to the staff shrink. As a matter of fact, the stress is one of the reasons I'm leaving this branch of social work at the end of the month." She watched as his gaze drifted out the car window. Then he turned his head and looked at her.

"I can't stop thinking that the collapse of the staircase could be my fault."

Annie thought about that for a minute. "I don't understand why," she finally said. "You were always so careful with safety features. Your boss at Belton's used to harangue you all the time about being overcautious."

"But maybe I wasn't this time."

"You were vigilant with these plans, Zach. Particularly because they were so innovative. I was there. I remember."

"With the plans maybe. But I'm afraid I blew it during the construction."

"Why?"

"Annie, you don't want to hear this. It has to do with us."

"How?"

Zach let out an exasperated breath. "Okay, just don't think I'm laying any guilt on you. I take full responsibility for our breakup."

"What does the building have to do with us?"

"I was a wreck when our marriage fell apart. I supervised the construction of that museum in the blackest mood I've ever had. Sometimes I hurt so much I couldn't think straight."

She hadn't known that, and the knowledge gripped her heart. She thought about how the Pierce Museum's design had been both lauded and criticized. She remembered Zach's assurance to his detractors that if erected properly, the building would be safe. She'd lost touch with the construction, of course, since the museum went up as their marriage ended. But she remembered some things well.

Zach's scrupulous attention to safety regulations.

Zach's consultations with the best engineers—at his own cost—about the structure's stability.

Zach's refusal to bow to the pressure to cut even the smallest corner.

"The disaster isn't your fault," she said implacably.

"Thanks for believing in me," he told her. "And for being here."

"Zach, why don't you come home with me for a while. I think you could use some company."

She'd repeated those words until he agreed. At her house, he'd gone into the living room as she fixed them something to eat. She wanted to do something—anything—to forget the death and destruction they had just witnessed.

When she came to the doorway from the kitchen, he was on the couch, staring blindly at the unlit fireplace. Her heart constricted at his hunched shoulders and bowed head. "Zach? Are you all right?"

"I…" He coughed to clear his throat. "I'm fine."

"Zach."

He sat perfectly still, hands fisted on his knees, his face averted.

She crossed to the couch and knelt in front of him. "You're crying." At that moment, all she wanted in the world was to take away his pain.

"I'm sorry…I just can't…"

"No, no, never be sorry for crying." Without thinking through what she was doing, she brushed her lips over his wet cheeks…once, twice, several times. "Look at me."

Opening his eyes, he stared at her.

"I know how hard it is to stop thinking about the tragedy," she said. Very slowly, her arms went around him. She drew him close. "Sometimes it feels as if the images will never go away."

Burying his face in her breasts, he said, "Annie, oh, God, Annie…"

"Shh…it's okay."

His arms banded around her waist.

He pulled her tight against his chest. "Annie…"

"Don't say anything."

He looked up at her.

Bombarded by the memories of bruised and broken bodies, Annie was overwhelmed by a need to drive them from her mind to affirm that she and Zach were all right. She forgot about all the pain they'd caused each other; she forgot that she'd been contemplating marrying someone else. All she thought about was comforting Zach and herself. All she felt was an acute and driving need for him. Her mouth on his cheek, her hands running up his back, tangling with the hair at his nape, she said, "Zach, *we're* all right, *we're* not hurt. Let's concentrate on that. Let's celebrate that."

"Oh, God, Annie, I need you so much."

That was why she'd done it, she thought, looking

around the reception area, trying to make sense of what had happened that night. She'd done it for them both. But she'd been surprised at the physical explosion that had occurred between them after so long…

Their first kiss in more than five years had been both ravenous and reverent. Her body reacted with a jolt to the press of his lips on hers, the familiar taste and texture of him. He sipped at her mouth, then devoured her, bathed her lips with his tongue and sucked greedily. They'd shed their clothes quickly. His hands caressed her stomach, her hips, gently at first. Then they clutched at her, grasped her almost roughly.

Her hands, too, sought the much-missed feel of his muscles, the sinewed strength of his arms, his legs, his chest.

When she found herself on her back, his lips made their way to one of his favorite spots on her body, the little patch of freckles on her chest, then he'd kissed his way to a mole on the outer curve of her right breast. The caress of his lips sent a rush of moisture between her legs, making her shiver. He moved a hand there.

His mouth came back to hers and brushed across it. His voice was hoarse when he whispered, ''Oh, Annie, you still respond to me so fast, so strongly. I've never forgotten it.''

''Neither have I.''

''I haven't forgotten anything.''

"Show me." Without any inhibition, she arched beneath him. "Come inside me."

His eyes were blue fire.

Never releasing her gaze, he guided himself to her and poised himself at her opening. Then he linked both hands with hers, establishing the familiar connection they shared every time they'd made love in the past. She felt her eyes fill, and saw moisture glisten in his. He entered her with a sure, possessive stroke. "Annie, love, nothing in my whole life has ever felt like this."

A sense of volcanic peace, he'd once poetically described it...

Just then the elevator doors opened. Several men stepped off. Jolted back to the present, Annie stood. The abrupt action caused the world to spin and she clutched the arm of the couch. Through hazy eyes, she caught sight of shoulders she'd recognize anywhere. Clothed in navy wool, they were big and broad and she had the absurd urge to curl into them and cry.

"Zach," Annie called out.

Zach pivoted and stared at her. In shock. *Oh, just wait.*

"Annie?" He walked toward her. Inches away, he stopped.

And right before her eyes, he withdrew. He folded his arms over his chest, and his blue eyes turned from curious to hostile. His jaw hardened. Annie had always hated his ability to retreat from her so completely, a technique he'd perfected as a young boy. Though she didn't blame him this time. She'd kicked him out of her life a second time four weeks ago and it had hurt him as much as it had hurt her. Only a masochist would welcome another shot at that kind of pain.

"What can I do for you?" His tone was cool and purposely distant.

"I need to talk to you."

He scanned her rumpled dress and messy hair, his eyebrows forming a V. "Are you all right?"

She shook her head. Some of his reserve melted. She could see it in the softening around his eyes. He always was good when the chips were down.

"Come on back to my office," he said. Stepping away, he allowed her to pass. He raised his arm as if to touch her shoulder, then changed his mind.

As she walked beside him, Annie forced back the panic that rose inside her. She dreaded telling him about her pregnancy, remembering how much of Zach's outlook on life had been formed by the burden of caring for his numerous younger siblings. The first of eight children, Zach was five years older than the second Sloan child, and seventeen years older than the last. He'd helped to care for most of them as infants and toddlers, right through their childhood, and he'd made up his mind never to have children of his own. Then his uncle Cary had made things worse when he moved back to Lansing and took his fifteen-year-old nephew under his wing and shown him what life without kids could be like. For an impressionable teenage boy, it wasn't hard to choose which life he preferred.

Once Zach and Annie reached the reception area, they walked down a plushly carpeted corridor with subtly striped wallpaper and muted lighting. When she entered his office, the exquisite design took her breath away. His architectural genius was evident in the various slopes of the ceiling, the gleaming wood trim, the rounded desk and chairs that seemed to grow out of the walls and floor. To her right, a row of windows overlooked downtown Lansing's modest skyline. Annie bet the rent on this office was more than she'd paid for her whole house.

When she turned toward him, her already-nervous stomach lurched. His face had hardened again. A memory surfaced like a snake waiting to strike…

Damn it, Annie. I'm only twenty-five. I don't want to be a father yet. How could you forget to take the pills?

I got busy with this group of kids—

No. As usual, you got obsessed with your work and strung yourself out so tight that you can't think straight. You'd better not be pregnant…

Fine. We'll just sleep in separate rooms for the rest of the month, to make sure it doesn't happen in the meantime.

She hadn't been pregnant then, and she'd slept in the spare room for one night before he begged her to come back to bed with him, and she'd flown right into his arms…

He'd be furious at her now for getting pregnant. God knew what he'd ask her to do. To his baby. Would he want her to have… The thought made her stomach churn. "Zach, can I…where's the bathroom?"

As soon as he pointed to double wooden doors, Annie flew through them. She reached the toilet just in time and sank to her knees.

When she was done, she felt gentle flexing fingers on her shoulders. Tears welled in her eyes.

"Annie, sweetheart, are you okay?"

She nodded, keeping her head down.

"Are you done?"

Again the silent concurrence.

Tugging her up, he led her to a chair in the corner of the spacious bathroom and eased her down. He studied her for a minute, then went to the sink and wet a washcloth. When he returned, he hunched down in front of her, steadying her with one strong hand on her collarbone. Slowly he swabbed her face. The water was cool and soothing. She closed her eyes and moaned.

When he finished, he smoothed the hair off her cheek, letting his hand linger in the heavy mass. "Want to brush your teeth?"

She opened her eyes. He was looking at her with such tenderness she wanted to cry. "Yes."

Straightening, he retrieved toothpaste, brush and mouthwash from a cabinet. "Need some help?"

"No, I can do it. I'll be right out."

With one long look at her, he closed the bathroom door.

ZACH WAS MYSTIFIED. He crossed to the window and stared out at downtown Lansing. What was going on here? What was wrong with Annie? And why the hell did he care?

He hadn't seen her since four weeks ago when, after she'd made passionate love to him, she'd told him she'd wanted nothing to do with him. In the last twenty-eight days the pain of losing her a second time, combined with the slow progress of the investigation into the collapse of the museum staircase, had Zach thinking he might well lose his mind. He clenched his fist, resisting the urge to pound on the glass. Was anything ever going to be right in his life again?

Staring out the window, he was still haunted by the events of the night he last saw his ex-wife. First, there'd been the heart-stopping news that the Pierce Museum staircase—the most spectacular aesthetic feature in all of his designs—had collapsed. Paralyzed with shock and fear, Zach had gripped the phone when the city planner had called him to ask for the blueprints. Then, seeing the inside of his building in ruins. And finally, the victims. Oh God! The victims...

Zach had been unable to leave once the stabilizing efforts had been implemented. Slightly panicked, he'd sought out Annie. "What can I do now?" he asked her.

"Nothing. Go home, Zach. Thanks for your help. I'll call you when we learn anything important."

He'd been instantly angry. Did she think he could just walk away from a tragedy that might be his fault?

It hit him with sledgehammer impact. That's exactly what she thought of him. That's exactly what she'd *always* thought of him. It still hurt. "I'm not leaving, Annie. I want to stay and help."

For an hour, he'd assisted the rescuers. He was near the front of the building when a shout came from within.

"Someone's stuck," a rescuer called out. "We need help in here."

Zach followed three firemen into the building.

Inside, there was a hazy, powdery feel in the air—drywall that had split apart, sawdust from where the chain saws had cut away the large pieces the rescuers couldn't move. His eyes felt gritty immediately and his mouth dried.

"Over here," a fireman called. Zach sidestepped the oak and brass of the staircase. Off to the side, three men worked at unpiling several wooden beams.

"Here, take this," a man said, shoving a crowbar into Zach's hands. "You pry from that end, I'll go from here, while Joe uses the pulley."

Together, they applied pressure. Zach's muscles strained and he spread his legs to give himself better leverage. Finally a large joist budged. Then the men attacked the smaller pieces of wood and glass and plaster. Zach pitched in. Though he'd donned a pair of gloves, he felt something jagged rip though them, but he ignored the accompanying pain. He could hear the shrill of the chain saws from the opposite side of the staircase, and glass breaking floors above him.

Finally they reached the victim.

Zach froze. A woman's body lay squashed beneath a beam that was buried with her. Her head lolled to one side and her mouth hung open. Zach didn't need a doctor's diagnosis to know.

She was dead…

"Zach."

Abruptly, he came back to the present. Turning, he faced a pale, trembling Annie in the doorway. He focused on her to regain his composure. He stared at her, trying not to reveal how much just seeing her again hurt. The memory of how that night four weeks ago had ended was vivid. They'd made love—passionate, almost desperate love. And Zach had told her he wanted another chance with her…

I've changed since we split up. So have you, I can tell.

Maybe I have. Maybe you have. Be we can't be sure. Or if it's enough.

We could try.

No, I can't take that risk.

You mean you won't *take the risk.*

All right, I won't…

Annie was still standing in the doorway.

"Sit down," he said.

Gingerly she found a chair and sank into it. He was disconcerted by the effort that motion seemed to take. Looking up at him, she said, "I've followed the news about the building."

"The press is having a field day. Especially Jonathan Gumby."

"Who's he?" Annie asked.

"A reporter who seems to have a special interest in architectural safety."

"I'm sorry. It must be hard, not knowing." He nodded. "Is the Occupational Health and Safety Administration still looking at the blueprints and specs?"

"Yep. I've gone over them with a fine-tooth comb. I'll be surprised if they find anything."

"You look tired."

He shoved his hands in his pockets. "I haven't slept well in the last few weeks."

"Because of the building."

"Among other things." He tracked the lines of strain in her face. "Why are you here? If you're this sick, you should be home in bed."

She said nothing, just looked at him. Of all the things about Annie that had first attracted Zach almost fifteen years ago, it was her eyes that he was craziest about. They were big and wide and thickly lashed. Mostly they were the color of fall leaves, but when she was angry or aroused, they turned green.

"Do you need something from me?"

She bit her lip. She always did that when she was afraid to tell him something. Had she come to give him bad news? Oh God, was she getting married?

"I'm pregnant, Zach."

Reflexively he sucked in a breath. He grasped the nearest object...the edge of his teak desk. Her announcement was the last thing he expected. The thought that she'd slept with someone after... Wait a minute. He checked his Rolex. April thirtieth. The staircase collapsed on March twenty-ninth. Four weeks ago.

Certain realities flicked into focus. Stripping off her clothes and his...sinking to the floor...he'd used no condom, no protection. He'd thought about that night every single day since then, fantasized about it, cursed it. But never once had he dreamed...

"It's my baby."

She nodded, her eyes wide and apprehensive.

"You're pregnant with my baby."

She swallowed. "Yes."

"*My* baby."

Again she nodded. He closed his eyes, but heard her say, "Look, Zach, I know this isn't what you want. And I understand why—about how you grew up. You won't have any responsibility for this child. That's not why I came. I just thought you had a right to know."

When he found the strength to open his eyes, he watched her carefully for a moment. Crossing to her slowly, he knelt at her feet, linked his hands with hers and tilted his head until his forehead met hers. "You're having my baby."

Annie had gone still. "Yes."

"When?"

"December thirty-first."

He drew back. "Our anniversary."

She didn't say anything.

Looking down at her stomach, he unlocked one hand and placed it over her belly. "My baby. Oh, God, Annie, this is wonderful."

Her whole body stiffened. He felt her hand clench in his, and then she yanked it away. With surprising strength, she pushed on his chest, forcing him back from her.

"Wonderful? You think this is wonderful?"

He smiled.

"You're glad? How can you be glad?"

"What do you mean?"

"What do I mean?" Her voice had risen. "Zach, the biggest problem we had was that you didn't want any kids. And your anger that I did led to other things—like Gina." She choked out the reference to his betrayal, and he winced. "Maybe we could have gotten past everything else, but not that. Now you're telling me you're *happy* about becoming a father? I can't believe it."

Sighing, he sat on the couch next to her. When he

reached for her, she shrugged him off and stood. "No, don't touch me. I can never think straight when you touch me."

He smiled. At least that hadn't changed. Despite all their differences, there was one area where they were perfectly, exquisitely matched. Nothing in his entire life—before or since—had brought him as much joy, as much peace, as being physically connected to her.

"Zach, how can you be happy about this pregnancy? It's a mistake."

"You think our baby is a mistake?"

That deflated her and she swayed on her feet. He rose to steady her again, grasping her arms, touching the woman who had haunted his sleep for almost fifteen years.

"I thought that's what *you'd* say," she whispered brokenly, resting her head on his shoulder.

"No, honey, it's wonderful."

Annie shook her head. "I don't understand."

"I've changed, Annie." His arms came around her. "I tried to tell you that four weeks ago. I've learned from the past."

She looked up at him with huge, vulnerable eyes. "You want this baby?"

"More than I can express."

"I never expected this."

"Well, it's true."

He watched her regroup. Drawing away, she squared her shoulders and shook her hair back. It was so typical of Annie. Taking things on the chin, finding a way to deal with them.

Except for Gina.

He shoved Gina out of his mind.

"So, where do we go from here?" he asked as lightly as he could, given that his pulse was beating double time.

She took a deep breath. "Well, all right. When she's born, you can be part of her life. That'll be good," Annie said slowly, as if trying to convince herself. "She won't grow up like I did, not knowing her father."

"She? Do you know we're having a girl?"

Annie gave him one of those subtle smiles that used to turn him inside out. "In my heart. It's too soon to tell any other way."

He smiled back and her eyes widened.

That grin could get you anything you want from me, Zachary Sloan, she'd once told him. He was ashamed of how much he'd used it to make her bend to his will.

She drew back as if she'd had the same thought. "I'll call you when she's born. We'll work something out."

Decisively she started to walk past him.

He caught her arm. "Not so fast. That's not enough."

"What do you mean?"

Crossing his arms over his chest, he said, "I think we should get remarried right away."

Annie froze. "No, absolutely not."

"Why not? You're carrying my child."

"That's not enough reason to remarry. We're too different. We had too many problems we couldn't work through."

Zach reached out to touch her stomach. "We have more reason to work through them now."

For long seconds, she stared at him. Her eyes filled with remembered pain. "You can't expect me to forget what you did. It hurt so much…" She shook off the emotion and tilted her chin. "I won't risk it again." Before he could protest, she said stonily, "Don't push me on this. Don't make me sorry that I told you."

He let it go. For now. "All right. But I want to be part of the pregnancy and the birth."

Her jaw dropped. "What? Why?"

"I've read about bonding. I want to be in this right from the beginning."

"Oh, Zach, I don't know."

"Besides, you look as if you could use some help. A stiff wind could blow you over."

As if on cue, her stomach rolled and she brought her hand to it. He caught her by the shoulders and gently pulled her down to the couch. "Annie, honey, it's obvious that you need someone. Let it be me."

Again she seemed to deflate before his eyes. Her weakness worried him. He drew her into a loose embrace, his hand threading through her hair. Would his child inherit those glorious auburn curls?

"I don't know Zach," she said. "I'm not sure. I..."

"Shh." He kissed the top of her head. "At least for today, let me take care of you."

"I haven't let anyone take care of me since you and I split."

Another piece of good news. "Well, then, let me take care of my baby." He rose, bringing her with him. "Did you drive here?"

"No, I was too sick. I took the bus."

"Come on, then, I'm taking you home. We'll talk more after you've rested."

She looked as if she wanted to protest, but her pallor told him she didn't have the energy.

Thank God for her acquiescence, he thought tenderly as he led her though his offices to his car. *And for this baby she's carrying.*

Because he wasn't going to let her go again.

CHAPTER TWO

ANNIE LAID her head back on the cushiony seat of Zach's car and closed her eyes, hoping he would think she was asleep. She knew she was taking the coward's way out, but she had to get control of herself before they got home. Disconcerted by his joy about the baby, she needed all her wits about her to deal with this newest development. If only she wasn't so weak…and so affected by Zach's presence. She looked down through slitted eyes to see her hands trembling. Proximity to Zach had always reduced her to quivering, and apparently time hadn't dulled her response.

She'd been only eighteen when she'd met him. Zach had gone to MIT, she to a girls' school down the road from the university. It was common practice in the eighties to bus the girls from Saint Mary's to MIT for fraternity parties. The first time she'd seen him sweet-talk a girl up to his room, her trouble detector had gone off. She decided to ignore him. It had worked for a while. He told her later he knew enough to stay away from her, too.

Then came that accidental meeting that changed her life…

"What you looking for, little girl?" A deep male voice had startled her in the stacks of a musty old section of the MIT library and she dropped the small piece of paper she was holding.

"You scared me."

Zach bent down to pick up her note.

"I, um, need a book on human behavior. I'm a first-year student at Saint Mary's."

"I know." Glancing at the paper, he said, "S-904.3." He scanned the stack in front of her, then plucked the volume from a high shelf. Skimming the title, he laughed, deep and from the belly. *"The Sexual Practices of Ancient African Tribes?"*

Cursed with fair skin to match her red hair, she felt herself blush. His eyebrows furrowed and he stopped laughing when he saw her embarrassment. It had been one of the things that had ultimately attracted her to Zach—his sensitivity toward others. A popular baseball player and sophisticated senior, he never ridiculed anyone, and often stepped in when his friends made fun of others. "Hey, it's okay." He frowned at the book he held. "You don't go to MIT. How you gonna check this out?"

"I'm not. I'm going to stay here and take notes."

"Tell you what. Have coffee with me at the union and I'll check the book out for you. You can read it on your own time."

Every self-protective instinct in Annie surfaced, and she stepped back, about to say no. But his blue eyes were dark and sincere, and he gave her a boyish grin that tipped the scales.

"All right."

In the student union, he was as dangerous as she knew he'd be. His broad shoulders, outlined in a plain navy polo shirt, made her pulse quicken. They talked for two hours; she was entranced by his intelligence, wit and maturity. But it was his Humphrey Bogart, John Wayne, Gary Cooper persona that really got to her. A die-hard fan of old movies, Annie loved the tough-guy-who-just-needed-the-love-of-a-good-woman story line.

When it grew late, he glanced at his watch. "Come on, I'll drive you to your dorm."

Alarm skittered through her. "Um, no, thanks. I'll take the bus."

"Can't. They aren't running anymore. Since it's my fault you missed your ride, I'll see you home safely."

Safe? With Zachary Sloan. She'd be as safe with him as she'd be with Don Juan. But she had little choice. "All right."

In his battered '79 Ford, she stayed far to the right in the front seat. She'd known for six months that he was bad news for her.

He swerved into a parking space at the dorm and cut the engine. In the sudden silence, she could hear his windbreaker rustle. Turning toward her, he raised his arm to the back of the seat and softly spoke her name. She whipped her head around, the nervous action sending her hair flying. Long, curly auburn locks covered his arm…and snagged in his watchband. When she tried to yank away, a jolt of pain shot from her scalp through her body. "Ouch."

"Easy," he said with exasperation. "Let me help." He slid over in the seat and gently untangled the heavy strands. Only to fist his hand in the red mass.

"I've never seen anything like this. It's so thick…and silky." He raised the waist-length hair to his nose and inhaled. "It smells like roses."

Annie gulped, mesmerized by the feel of his hand in her hair and the husky tenor of his voice. She watched as he lifted his other hand to the curve of her cheek. Delicately, he traced the bridge of her nose down either side of her face. "These freckles beg to be kissed." Running his thumb over her bottom lip, he said, "So do these." His voice rough, he asked, "Can I kiss you, little girl?"

She shook her head.

He repeated the last caress. "Just once? I've been wondering what you'd taste like for months."

Her eighteen-year-old heart expanded at his flattery. She nodded.

Annie had been kissed before, many times, but never like this—practiced, polished and primed for seduction. She fell into it helplessly. But halfway through, something changed.

Zach's lips became more urgent. His hands shook. He moaned.

Thrilled by her first taste of female power, she raised her arms to his neck and leaned into him.

Annie never knew how long they would have kissed or how far they would have gone if a group of coeds hadn't walked by the car, pounded on the hood and teased, "You're fogging up the windows."

They sprang apart like adulterers.

Raising a shaky hand to her mouth, Annie saw Zach's chest heave, and she noticed two buttons on his shirt were undone. His eyes were blazing with unsuppressed desire. She moved toward the door. His strong hand grasped her shoulder.

"Wait," he said raggedly.

She stopped and turned away.

"What happened here?"

She shook her head, her back to him.

"Annie, turn around." His voice gentled. When he tugged on her arm, she swiveled to face him. He said, "I know you don't do this kind of thing regularly."

"How do you know that?"

"The guys at the frat house...they talk."

"Oh? And what do they say?"

"That no one's gotten to first base with you."

"So? Is something wrong with that?"

"No, of course not. But how do you explain this?" His gesture encompassed the interior of the car.

"I don't have to explain this." She reached for the door handle.

He stopped her again. "Whoa, sweetheart. I want some answers. You just melted in my arms. If those girls hadn't come by…"

Annie glared at him. "It goes both ways, hotshot. I wasn't the only one who almost lost it."

"I know. That's why I've avoided you for six months."

"Well, avoid me for six more. We've got to be the most mismatched couple on these two campuses. You're way out of my league, Zach."

"Because you're a virgin?"

"Not only that, but…" She frowned, realizing what she'd admitted.

"You are, aren't you?"

"That's none of your business."

"It was, a few minutes ago." He sighed, then shook his head. "Look, I don't know why I'm arguing about this. You're right. We're oil and water."

Annie had been oddly disappointed, and vastly relieved. Scrambling for her pride, she opened the door. "Well, that settles it then. Thanks for the lift…and the book. I'll be sure to return it."

Staying away from each other had worked—for two months. Until one Friday night. She was at a party. Zach had a gorgeous date. Annie remembered being jealous as hell. She'd had a few beers, but was far from drunk. One of Zach's frat brothers started hitting on her and she flirted back. Apparently, that was all Zach needed to see. He left his date literally openmouthed, stalked over to Annie and practically dragged her out of the house to his car. They'd been inseparable after that...

Now, fifteen years later, Annie looked across the front seat at Zach, studying his chiseled profile in the stark April sunlight. The Jag pulled into her driveway and she watched Zach swing easily out of the low-slung car. As he circled the front and opened the door for her, she couldn't forget how unexpectedly he'd come through for her, at least temporarily, about the baby.

Watch it, Annie, don't get carried away. Just because he didn't throw a fit doesn't mean he's like...Peter.

Peter. Her almost-fiancé. Oh, God, she hadn't thought about Peter all morning. Four weeks ago she'd been contemplating marriage to Peter, a sweet kind man who was the opposite of Zach. A man who didn't deserve the pain she was going to cause him.

Without comment, she got out of the car and walked to the front of her quaint little Victorian house in a middle-class neighborhood of Lansing. When she opened the ornate door and stepped into the foyer, she was knocked backward into Zach's arms by one hundred and fifty pounds of dog. "Daisy. Down, girl."

The mostly-Lab's ears perked up and her paws skidded on the slate floor of the foyer as she tried to get around Annie.

Moving aside, Annie watched as man and beast participated in a tender reunion. Daisy was all over

Zach. She licked his face and sniffed every part of
him she could reach. When he dropped to one knee
and buried his nose in Daisy's neck saying, "Hiya,
girl," Annie turned away...

Oh, Zach, look at her.

She's a mutt, Annie.

I want her.

Why?

*If I can't have a baby now, at least let's get a
pet....*

Biting her lip, Annie hurried away from the foyer,
away from the memory, away from the man. She
tossed her purse and keys on a chair and said, "I've
got to take Daisy out."

Zach stared at her. "I didn't know you still had
her," he said softly. "Where was she the night of
the collapse?"

"I leave her with the boy next door when I know
I'm not going to be home to let her out."

He smiled sadly. "I...I missed her."

Daisy barked, and Annie and Zach both smiled.

"She obviously missed you, too," Annie said
thoughtfully. "You didn't want her at first."

"Yeah. I'd taken care of pets and kids all my life.
It's one of the reasons I couldn't wait to leave
home."

"I never knew that was why you objected to taking her."

He gave her a smile that clutched her heart. "Remember the time she ate my Italian loafers?"

"Yes, I remember."

His eyes glittered with sexual intensity. "Do you remember all of it?"

Annie did. "Why don't you take her out?" she said, avoiding the issue. "I need to lie down."

But once in her bedroom, Annie couldn't stop the memory. As she got into a sweat suit, she remembered the Italian loafers...

Zach had been getting ready for an important work dinner, one where he was trying to impress a client. Dressed in unzipped trousers, he was fishing for his shoes in the small closet.

"Damn it."

"What's the matter?" Annie had been keeping him company while he dressed, brushing her hair, sitting cross-legged on their bed in her underwear.

"I can't find one of my Italian loafers. Do you know where they are?"

Just then, Daisy bounded through the open door. With his shoe in her mouth. Annie laughed and Zach let out a string of obscenities, ending with, "Can't you teach her to behave?"

The laughter bubbled out of Annie. "I can't. You know those books I checked out on dog obedience?"

He glared at her. "Yeah?"

"She ate those, too. I had to pay the library for them."

Then she started to giggle, at the irony of Daisy's actions, at sexy Zach with unzipped pants holding a half-eaten loafer. At Daisy, staring adoringly at her master.

Zach began to laugh, too, and fell on the bed with Annie. He pinned her to the mattress and brushed her cheek with his knuckles. "You're so good for me, baby. You make me take myself not so seriously."

He'd been late for his appointment because he'd made tender love to her...

Annie was roused from the memory by the sound of Zach returning with Daisy. She lay down, waiting for him to come in. God, she was tired. She hadn't known pregnancy could make a woman so weak, physically and emotionally. And so fast. She was barely a month along and already she'd lost control of her body.

"Feel better?" he asked from the doorway.

"Yes, thanks. When I move around, my stomach's worse."

"Have you eaten today?"

She shuddered. "Don't even mention it."

He came farther into the room and eased onto the edge of the bed. "Annie, what did the doctor say about the nausea?"

"I have a midwife."

"A midwife?"

Annie sighed. "She's a board certified midwife, working in a doctor's office. I'll have the baby in a hospital, with plenty of care."

"What did she say about the sickness?"

"She said it's common. A lot of women get sick in the early stages."

"This sick?"

"Yes."

His scowl was fierce. "I don't like it. I'm going to call someone else."

"No, Zach, don't."

"Why?"

"There's no reason to bring in anyone else."

"I want another opinion," he said implacably.

"No. You're not going to barge in here and take over."

"Well, I'm not going to sit back and watch you waste away, either."

"Don't bully me, Zach."

The comment brought back an old argument...

You do too much, Annie. You let this job wear you out.

I do too much? You're the workaholic.

I don't run myself into the ground.

Don't bully me, Zach...

His forehead creased as he watched her. She could see the wheels turning.

"And don't try to manipulate me. You may be the father of this baby, but I'm no longer your wife."

"A fact that I regret more than I can say."

Because she felt so queasy, and because she felt so vulnerable, she snapped at him. "All right, let's get this straight right now. You can be part of the baby's life. You're entitled to that. You're even entitled to be part of the pregnancy and birth, if you want. But you're not entitled to me. To taking care of me, making decisions for me, running my life. Is that clear?''

His jaw clenched. ''Yes, it's clear. But how can I take care of my baby without taking care of you?''

My baby. Why did he have to keep saying that? It sounded so…intimate.

A wave of fatigue washed over her without warning, as it did several times a day. She sank into the pillows and closed her eyes. She was afraid she was going to cry. Damn, her emotions had always been close to the surface. She cried at television commercials and at songs on the radio. Apparently, pregnancy was going to turn her into a weeping idiot.

''Annie, I'm sorry. I came here to help. Not to badger you.''

She opened her eyes. ''I know. I'm sorry, too. My emotions careen out of control more than usual.''

Brushing his knuckles over her cheek, he grazed her lips with the pad of his thumb. It felt good. ''You're entitled.''

She smiled gratefully.

''My mother used to eat saltine crackers every time she got pregnant,'' he said. ''Let me get you some of those, and maybe some tea.''

''Okay. There's crackers in the pantry and decaffeinated tea bags in the cupboard. Use those.'' She grabbed his arm when he started to rise. ''Zach, before you go…I have to ask you something.''

"What?"

"You'll get mad."

"No, I won't. I promise."

"We didn't use any protection that night."

"Obviously. It never entered our minds." His grin was filled with sexual promise. "We had other… concerns."

"And I was on the Pill when we were together," she said, ignoring the innuendo. "Even though I missed taking them a few times, and we had to use something else, mostly we didn't." She took in a deep breath. "But condoms are for more than pregnancy prevention." At his puzzled look, she said, "I hate to ask you this, but you must have dated a lot of women…"

His bright blue eyes dulled and she found it hard to go on.

"You don't have to ask," he finally said. "I…ah…" He got up and paced. He ran a hand through his hair. "I hadn't been with a woman for six months before the collapse of the staircase. Two weeks ago, I had a physical exam. Everything— blood work included—is fine." He came back to the bed and stared down at her. "Nothing's wrong with me that could hurt the baby."

"Why hadn't you been—"

Leaning over, he pressed two fingers to her lips. "Shh. I'll go get the crackers and tea."

Wearily, Annie closed her eyes, fearful of what

was happening, knowing how dangerous it was to depend on Zach for anything.

IN THE KITCHEN Zach rummaged through the cupboards and pantry until he found the tea and crackers. As the water heated, he looked around the small, quaintly decorated room. It was so typical of Annie. And so unlike him. Just like everything else...

Zach, you paid four hundred dollars for that suit?... A country club... Us?... I don't care what happened, you've got to go see your family... Please, Zach, I want your baby so badly...

Sighing, he spotted flowers on the table. Pink and white carnations. Annie's favorites. He remembered one time he'd filled the bedroom with them after they'd had a fight, and they'd made love—several times—amidst the fragrant scent.

Who'd sent them to her? Crossing to the table, he picked up the card. *Hope you feel better. Peter.*

Peter? The name rang a bell. Zach remembered one of the workers and a couple of the firemen on the night the staircase collapsed asking Annie about him. Anger, fast and furious, sprang up within Zach. Someone else was sending his pregnant wife flowers. He stalked into the bedroom. She was leafing through a magazine.

"Who's Peter?" he asked, his teeth clenched.

She looked at him warily. "How do you know about Peter?"

"Well, the flowers, for one thing."

"He's a friend." She raised her chin, the way she used to when she was about to confront him. "Actually, we were talking about getting married."

Zach gripped the doorjamb. "Annie," he said, the sudden realization making his stomach churn. "If you were almost engaged, how do you know this is my baby?"

Her face turned pink. "Peter's been out of the country for almost three months setting up a Sister City relief program. It's a new thing with the Red Cross."

"I see." *Thank God.*

In the ensuing silence, she added, "I met him through work. He's a coordinator in Boston for overseas relief efforts."

"A noble profession."

Her chin hitched another notch. "Yes, it is."

"Just what you always wanted in a man."

"That's right."

Stifling the urge to punch his fist through the wall, Zach glanced around the room. "Does he live here with you?"

"No."

"How come?"

She shrugged. "Lots of reasons...."

I wish we could live together, Zach. I hate it when you drop me off at the dorm and go back to the frat house.

All right, I'll get an apartment the rest of the semester...

He watched her. "Tell me one thing. Are you going to marry him while you're carrying my baby?"

"Of course not. I just haven't wanted to tell him on the phone. He should be back in two weeks."

Unable to let it go, even now that he had the answer he wanted, Zach asked, "How long have you known him?"

She fidgeted with the sheet. "About two years."

They'd been divorced five years.

"Then there have been others?"

"Other what?"

"Lovers."

"That's none of your business."

Zach felt the anger burn inside him. "It's always been my business. I've never..."

"Zach, don't."

"One New Year's Eve..."

She leaned back into the pillows. "Our anniversary."

"Two years after we split, I came here."

She shook her head. "No, no, you didn't."

"Yes, but I didn't come to the door."

"Why?"

"There was a car in the driveway."

"Oh."

"I waited. Parked on the street. All night. He left about nine in the morning."

Annie shuddered.

"Annie?"

"It was...it was the first time I slept with anyone

else but you." She sucked in a breath. "I cried afterward."

The image of her crying tore at him. "I'm so sorry. For all of it."

Slowly she turned to face him. "Are you?"

"Yes."

"Then let's drop this right now. I'm exhausted."

"All right. I'll go get your tea."

When he returned, she was asleep. He deposited the snack on her dresser, eased down her pillow so she was lying flat and went to the windows to close the blinds. Then he sank onto a chair in the corner and watched her sleep, trying to take in how his life had changed in the last few hours.

Annie was pregnant with his child. What had he done to deserve this gift? Only hours ago he'd wondered if anything was ever going to go right again in his life. A baby. His and Annie's baby.

How ironic. He didn't delude himself that he'd been anything but unbending about having kids when they were together. He'd been a bastard at times. He cringed when he remembered the details. *You'd better not be pregnant.* Now he was ashamed.

In the bleak days and weeks after she divorced him, he'd admitted to himself the mistakes he'd made with her. And apparently, his refusal to consider having kids had been their biggest obstacle.

Until Gina.

Ah, yes, Gina. But in a way, she'd been part of

that same issue. He and Annie had argued vehemently that fateful day...

What kind of a man are you that you don't want any children?

I'm the same man you married.

No, no, you're not. The man I married just wanted to wait to have kids. You don't ever want any, do you?

No, I don't...

She'd looked at him then as if he had betrayed her. As always, her disapproval had been almost more than he could bear. It didn't excuse what he'd done with Gina, nothing ever could. He'd used Gina's flattery to boost his ego when Annie's condemnation had caused his self-esteem to plummet.

But in the five years since the divorce—and more dramatically since the museum disaster—he'd changed. He wanted different things from life. And now that he had a chance to show Annie, he was going to do it right this time.

Slowly, he got up and left the room. As he fed Daisy, the phone on the kitchen wall beckoned. Well, he'd changed, but not completely. She'd be mad at his interference, but her welfare was more important.

He dialed his junior partner's office.

"McCade here."

"Yeah, Devon, it's me, Zach."

"I'm glad you checked in. OSHA just called. They've made some decisions and want to meet with

you today at one o'clock. About the museum's collapse.''

"Did they give you any idea of their findings?"

"No."

"Okay. I'll call them back. Give me the number."

After he did, Devon asked, "Why did you call?"

Zach's heart swelled with the reminder that Annie
was having his baby. "Your brother's still practicing
medicine in Boston, isn't he?"

"Yeah, he just opened his own office."

"Do me a favor and call him. Find out who's the
best obstetrician in town. See if your brother can get
an appointment as soon as possible. Call me back
here." He dictated Annie's telephone number.

"Under whose name?" was Devon's only question.

"Annie Montgomery...Sloan."

THE OCCUPATIONAL SAFETY and Health Administration offices in downtown Lansing were unpreten-
tious, but that didn't ease Zach's anxiety. He'd been
waiting four long weeks for the board members to
come up with some plan of action, and now that they
had, his palms were sweaty.

"You can go in, Mr. Sloan," the receptionist told
him.

Zach gave her a weak smile as she ushered him
through a door marked Conference Room. Six men
sat around a huge table. Zach recognized some of the
faces.

"Good afternoon, Sloan," Tom Watson, the chief

officer of Lansing's division of OSHA, addressed him.

Mechanically, Zach shook his hand. Watson introduced the city engineers, whom Zach didn't know, the supervisor of Lansing's building-permits office, and the mayor, with whom Zach had worked several times. When Zach took a seat, he noticed the blueprints for the Pierce Museum spread out across the table. His gut clenched.

"We'll get right to the point," Watson said. "We've gone over these prints and all the other specs we can get our hands on. Several times."

"And?"

"We've met with the board of the museum, and with the insurance companies. Our decision is to test the steel-and-concrete beams leading from the foundation into the building's core."

Zach had been over those specs a thousand times. He knew they'd hold up. "Mind telling me why you decided to do this first?"

"It's the most logical place to start."

"I'd think you'd go aboveground first. The staircase should be scrutinized—the connections, the welding tests..."

"The whole building is controversial," the mayor said, his voice undercut with impatience.

"And," a city engineer put in, "the records show that the builder, Martin Mann, put in a request for a change order to increase the number of beams going into the structure."

"I denied the request," Zach said. "The number

and types of beams I designed would hold the building.''

"Well, maybe you were wrong, Sloan," the mayor said. "The newspapers speculated at the time that you were more concerned with aesthetics than safety."

Zach leaned forward, his eyes focused on the mayor. His voice was deadly cold. "I presented the owners with two separate expert opinions that those beams were enough. And after that newspaper article, I got a third firm to investigate. The building was delayed two months just to check that out."

No one spoke. Finally, Watson broke the charged silence. "Nevertheless, that's our decision."

Zach sat back and nodded. "All right. But I suggest you discuss what you're going to do next, because this isn't the problem." He stood. "If there's anything I can do, you know where to reach me."

With an air of confidence, Zach strode out of the office. But his stomach was in knots and his head was beginning to ache. As he stepped into the elevator, he was flooded with images of the collapse…breaking glass, the bruised limbs, the soft moans and piercing cries of the injured…the dead woman. As he pushed the button, he told himself to think of something else.

Annie. And his baby. He'd think about them.

ANNIE WAS CLEANING UP and worrying over the note Zach had left, when the front door opened. She heard Daisy's excited bark and Zach's soft murmurings.

When she entered the living room, he was on one knee, scratching Daisy's ears. He looked up, his face etched with lines of exhaustion, and her heart turned over.

"How'd it go?" she asked without preamble.

"Fine." He scanned her jeans and shirt. "Feeling better?"

"Yes. I ate some of the crackers and reheated the tea."

Patting the dog, he stood. Zach tugged at his tie as he set the key on the table by the foyer. "I took this because I didn't want to wake you when I returned."

Though she didn't like the idea of his rummaging through her house to find a key, she let it go. Her complaint seemed petty compared to what he might have discovered about the staircase collapse. "Thanks." She sat on a chair, studying him as he slumped on the couch, stretched out his legs, linked his hands behind his head and closed his eyes. She waited. Talking about his feelings had never been easy for Zach and she'd learned years ago not to rush him.

"They're going to start with the beams," he finally said.

"Which ones?"

"The columns—technically, they're called pilings—that go into the foundation."

"Did that surprise you?"

"No. It was the most criticized part of the design."

Annie smiled. "That and building it on a hillside."

A grin tugged at his mouth. "That, too."

"What do you think about the beams?"

"I know they were enough. Three independent engineering companies confirmed that."

"So why is OSHA checking them out first?"

"Because Martin Mann requested a change order to put in more beams than the design required, and I denied the order."

Annie cringed at the mention of the builder...

Zach, I don't like Martin Mann.

You don't like any of my business associates.

That's not true. I like the Corrigans. I wouldn't mind spending more time with them...

Shaking off the unpleasant memory, Annie asked, "Why did you deny the order?"

"Because it wasn't necessary. And Les Corrigan agreed with me. Mann bid the job with the original number of beams. A change order would have cost the owners thousands of dollars. And we would have had to widen the circumference of the foundation, which would have altered the whole appearance of the building. It wasn't necessary, so I said no."

"Why is your decision being questioned now?"

"At the time, some overeager reporter accused me of not wanting my design compromised. As if I'd sacrifice safety for aesthetics."

"You wouldn't do that."

"Thanks for the vote of confidence." He looked past her shoulder. "The reporter wasn't entirely wrong, though."

"About what?"

"I *didn't* want the aesthetics compromised."

"That doesn't matter, Zach, so long as you didn't take any chances."

"I didn't, Annie." He sat up straight and his hands fisted. "At least I don't think I did."

Hesitating only a moment, she crossed to the couch and sat down next to him. "Zach, you've got to have faith in your design and your integrity." She smiled. "I do."

"How can you say that, Annie? How can you have faith in my integrity after what I did to you?"

She knew he was talking about Gina. Annie battled back the pain. "I don't want to talk about Gina. Besides, they're two different issues." She stroked his hand, needing to touch him. "Tell me what will happen next."

"Not much for a while. The company that built the original beams will reconstruct them. Then they'll go to a lab where the same kind of stressors will be placed on them to see if they hold up. The stressors will have to be in place for a certain length of time."

"How long?"

"Months, I'd guess."

"That's a long time to wait." He didn't say anything. "You'll get through it, Zach."

"I'm worried about my company. The press has already speculated that I'm at fault. When this OSHA thing gets out, business is bound to slack off. The longer it goes on, the worse off we'll be."

"I'm sorry."

"Me, too." Giving her a weak grin, he placed a large masculine hand on her belly. Her stomach flip-flopped, not from morning sickness this time. "But now I have something else to think about."

She smiled. The phone rang. Reluctantly, she got up to answer it. "Hello?"

"I'd like to speak to Annie Sloan."

Her hand gripped the receiver at hearing the name she'd given up when she'd given up on Zach. "This is Annie. I go by Montgomery now."

"Oh. Well, Ms. Montgomery, we have an appointment for you to see Dr. Barry tomorrow at four o'clock."

"Dr. Barry? Who's Dr. Barry?"

There was a pause. "Chief of obstetrics at Boston Medical Center."

"I don't understand. I didn't—"

She hadn't heard Zach come up behind her. Gently, he took the phone from her. "Hello, this is Ms. Montgomery's husband. I called for the appointment. Can Dr. Barry see her soon?"

Annie watched openmouthed.

"Fine, we'll be there at four. Thanks for doing this on such short notice."

His movements unusually precise, Zach placed the phone in its cradle. He reached for her shoulders. "Let me explain this, honey."

She stepped back, arms wrapped around her shaky tummy. Oh, he'd changed all right! "Get out, Zach."

CHAPTER THREE

"GET OUT?" He stared at her. "You can't be serious."

"You just don't get it, do you?"

Zach struggled to hold on to his temper. Annie had always been able to trigger it quicker than anyone else in his life. "Don't you think you're overreacting? I just wanted you to get the best care."

"Zach, I told you to stay out of it. I don't want another opinion. I trust my midwife. You went expressly against my wishes by calling someone else."

"Why don't you want another opinion?"

"I don't need it."

"How do you know that?"

"This is my body. My choice. I'll make the decisions."

"It's my baby, too."

"Oh, stop saying that."

Zach bit back a retort at how that phrase seemed to irritate her. "It *is* my baby. Do you wish it was someone else's? Maybe Peter's?" he asked nastily.

"No, of course not."

Hallelujah. "Listen, Annie—"

"No, you listen. You can't just barge into my life after five years and start taking over again."

"I never took over before."

"You tried."

"You were too damn stubborn to let me. We worked it out anyway."

"We got divorced."

"Not over this."

"I'm not going to fight you on this issue, Zach. If you can't control that bullying streak, having you in the baby's life is never going to work."

His shoulders sagged. God, he was tired. And worried. In just a few short weeks, his whole professional life had been threatened, and in the last several hours, his personal life had been turned upside down. "All right. Tell me what you want."

"I want you to leave me alone."

She'd said that once before...

I want you to leave me alone. Take your lying heart and cheating body and get out of my life...

The thought sobered him. He couldn't lose her again. Desperate, he asked, "Do you really mean that, Annie?"

She started to speak, then stopped. Several emotions flickered across her lovely face. "No, I guess not," she finally said. "You're entitled to be part of this. *Part,* Zach, not the whole show."

"Okay," he said slowly. "Just let me be here for you."

Closing her eyes, Annie sighed. "I want you to

be. I'm scared. This is so new. I…I don't want to go through it alone.''

"I'm scared, too, honey." *Of losing you again.* He pulled her into a comforting embrace. She sank against him. He kissed the top of her head. "I'll try, Annie. I promise. I can be better. Please, give me a chance to show you that.''

She rested in his arms a moment, then drew away. "I don't know, Zach. I'm even more scared of giving you another chance to hurt me.''

"I won't hurt you again. I promise. Please, don't make any decisions now. You're exhausted, and confused. Let me help you out, let's get to know each other again, and see what happens. Please, Annie. Say yes.''

After a long pause, she put her hand on her stomach and looked up at him with those hazel eyes that could shred a man's self-control. "All right, Zach," she said in a voice he could barely hear. "Let's see what happens. For the baby and for us.''

ANNIE'S MOTHER lived in a loft. Sonya Montgomery had moved there five years ago when she'd come to Lansing to be near her daughter. At eight o'clock in the morning, Annie dragged herself up the third and final flight of stairs. She was grateful that she was between jobs, since the trek up the steps exhausted her. Having left Relief and Rescue last week, she was due to start at Family Services on Monday. She hoped four more days of rest would revive her enough so that her legs no longer felt like cooked noodles each time she exerted herself.

Annie took a deep breath as she rang the bell, shaking her head at the bright red front door with a heart wreath on it. On the second ring, Sonya whipped opened the door. "Annie, darling, I tried to call you ten minutes ago. Must be our auras are in sync."

Today, Sonya was decked out in psychedelic beads and a tie-dyed dress. The skirt flowed around her ankles. Barefoot, she looked as if she'd stepped straight out of the sixties. She wore her dark hair back in a long braid. Despite the fact that her hands were covered with dirt, she hugged Annie enthusiastically.

Jarred by the movement, Annie grasped the doorway as a wave of dizziness hit her.

Sonya drew back. "Are you all right?"

"Yes."

"Come on in." Annie followed her mother across the living area of the huge one-room dwelling. Sonya went to the kitchen-alcove sink. The loft was bright and airy, with long, wide windows. Covering the walls were vivid canvases of Sonya's modern art. Painting was the part-time profession that—along with money her grandmother had left her—had supported Sonya all her life. "I was tending to my herb garden." A profusion of green decorated the windowsill jutting out from the sink. "Have a seat."

Annie sat. Now that she was here, she was beginning to lose her nerve. There were...complications to telling Sonya she was pregnant, and Annie feared her mother's reaction. "How are you, Mom?" she asked, delaying the revelation.

Sonya fussed at the counter. "I've just made some tea and sourdough bread." She came to the table with a loaded tray and set it down. Annie's stomach lurched. "Darling, what's wrong? You've gone white."

Swallowing hard, Annie willed herself not to be sick again. "I'm all right."

Sonya pushed a cup in front of her daughter. "Here, it's your favorite kind. Peppermint and cinnamon."

Annie drew in a deep breath. "Take it away, Mom, will you?"

After Sonya cleared the table, leaving only a cup of tea for herself, she sat back down. "What is it, dear?"

"I'm not feeling well today." In the absence of food and tea smells, Annie's stomach relaxed.

Her mother's gray eyes darkened with concern. She reached out and took Annie's hand. "Have you seen a doctor?"

Annie bit her lip to keep from sighing. Another hurdle. Sonya was into natural health care and alternative healing methods. As soon as she heard about the baby, she'd have her own suggestions.

Just like Zach.

So Annie further delayed the inevitable. "I'm fine,

Mom. Tell me why you were calling me so early? Weren't you afraid you'd wake me up?''

"You never stayed in bed late in your life, darling. Except when Zachary kept you there, and I doubt you were sleeping.'' Her mother's delicate jaw tensed. "Actually, Zachary's the reason I called.'' From a low table by the window, Sonya produced a newspaper. "The news is not good, Annie. I wanted to be the one to tell you.''

Taking the *Lansing Gazette,* Annie flipped it open to the first page. The headlines read, Who's To Blame? OSHA's Focus: The Beams. Annie noted the byline. Jonathan Gumby. Then she scanned the article, glossing over the technical details that Zach had explained. Finally she zeroed in on the closing lines. "The collapse of the museum's staircase seems to support recent concern in the community and in the press about architects sacrificing safety for innovation. It's a possibility that cannot be ignored. Maybe the collapse of the Pierce will serve as a wake-up call.''

After what Zach had told her, Annie had been expecting the paper's attack. What she wasn't prepared for was the large photograph of Zach, more handsome than a cover model, in a tux, his hair a little messy, sporting that cocky, sexy grin that had gotten him into her heart quicker than a flash. The shot was taken at the opening of the museum. He was basking in praise. On his arm was a beautiful woman glittering in gold and sequins.

Annie's gaze traveled to the quote below: "The structure of the building is indeed radical. But I'm still positive, as I was when I built it, that it's safe. Something else went wrong." This was Zach's initial statement, made weeks ago. He'd refused comment since then.

When Annie's eyes caught Martin Mann's name, she shivered.

"I just don't know," the builder had told the reporter. "Sloan's the best architect around. But the design was radical. It's hard to tell. I'm sure everything will come out in the wash."

Yeah, and I hope it's your dirty laundry, you jerk.

"Well, at least you've got some color in your face. Zachary Sloan always did that for you."

Annie quelled the spurt of irritation she felt at Sonya's readiness to approve Zach. She said only, "You always were a sucker for his charm."

"He was good for you, Annie."

Of course, her mother never knew about Gina. Annie hadn't told her—it was too personal and too devastating. Only Zach's sister Lucy knew. One desperate night, Annie had blurted it out to Lucy, who was a close friend. Later, Annie had regretted the confidence, which had added to Lucy's exaggerated resentment of her brother. "Mom, why do you think Zach was so good for me? Surely you realized we fought about everything."

Sonya's eyes turned misty, the way they did when she meditated. "Maybe because he loved you so much, even though you were different. That kind of devotion is rare. It always made me sad that he was out of your life."

Well, Grandma, I'm about to make you a happy woman.

"I know you were. I've got something to tell you."

Sonya waited.

"I'm pregnant."

"Pregnant?"

Annie nodded.

"But I thought...I always hoped..." Her eyebrows furrowed. "Peter's been in South America for a few months, hasn't he?"

Annie blushed. "Yes."

Sonya just stared at her.

Tilting her head toward the newspaper, Annie said, "The night that building collapsed, I worked on the relief crew."

"I know. I was worried that it would be a painful reminder of Zach for you. The museum was his first big design."

"It *was* painful." She hesitated. "Mom, Zach was there. He brought the plans and helped with the rescue work afterward."

"I didn't know that. Why didn't you tell me?"

"You never could be objective about him."

"What happened to be objective about?"

"Zach was devastated, of course, by the collapse.'' Annie stared past her mother's shoulder. ''I brought him home with me.''

''Really?''

''He spent the night.'' She touched her stomach again. ''This is Zach's baby, Mom.''

The cup in Sonya's hand clattered to the table, spilling tea. Reaching for a napkin, she said, ''Oh my.'' When she lifted her eyes to her daughter, her whole face brightened. ''Why, darling, this is wonderful. It's exactly what you two need to bring you back together.''

''I'm not sure about that,'' Annie said.

''Does he know?''

''Yes, I told him right away.''

Slowly Sonya rose and carried her cup to the microwave. Annie watched as her mother put the cup in and turned on the machine. Finally Sonya came back to the table. ''You're smarter than I was. To tell him,'' she said as she sat down.

Annie stiffened. She loved her mother very much, eccentricities and all. But it had been difficult growing up with a parent like Sonya—her single-mother life-style, her absentmindedness, her odd appearance. But the most difficult thing was accepting that Sonya had never told Annie's father they were having a child. That still hurt.

''I thought it was best to tell Zach right away.''

''Because what I did wasn't best for you, was it?'' Sonya's eyes glistened.

Annie shook her head. ''No, Mom, it wasn't.''

"It seemed to be at the time. I was seventeen, and your father and I were so different. He had such big plans for his life. He wanted everything I didn't want. Zach's very much like him."

"Yes, I realize that. It always made me wonder why you liked Zach so much."

"Probably just for that reason. I made a mistake, Annie, not trying to work things out with your father. I hoped you wouldn't follow in my footsteps."

The admission surprised Annie. "Why didn't you ever tell me this?"

"I...I don't know. I'm not sure I even figured it out until you divorced Zach." Sonya straightened her shoulders. "Well, what are you going to do about the baby?"

"Nothing yet. I've been so sick I can barely think straight."

"What was Zachary's reaction?" Sonya's eyes narrowed. "I know he never wanted kids. Was he unpleasant about it?"

"No, he was elated."

Annie's mother laughed. "I always did like that boy."

"Aren't you surprised?"

"A little. Though I know for a fact he changed after you left him. He was beside himself when you split up."

Annie remembered how Zach had sought her mother's help after Annie had filed for divorce. "I know. And you sided with him."

"No, darling, he let me help him. You...closed yourself off from me."

"It was too painful to talk about, Mom."

"You never stopped loving him, did you?"

"No. And I've wanted a baby since I met him. His baby. I still feel that way."

"Well, it looks like fate has stepped in here, young lady. After all, if it's your destiny, you can't escape it."

Annie rolled her eyes.

"Now, about that morning sickness."

Annie held her breath.

"I know this wonderful Chinese masseuse who's had uncanny success with eliminating nausea and back pain."

ZACH PUT DOWN the folder on the latest job he was bidding and glanced at the clock. Four-fifteen. Annie would have been at the doctor's now, damn it, if she hadn't refused to go. He was so worried, he'd talked to her three times today. But he'd resisted the urge to stop at her house this morning, vowing not to smother her. She'd been on her way to Sonya's anyway. Sonya, his ally. There were two people who had helped him through the bleak days following the breakup with Annie—Sonya and Les Corrigan. His old friend had proved to be a staunch support.

The phone buzzed. "Yeah."

"Zach, it's the *Lansing Gazette* again," Mrs. Farnum, his secretary, told him.

He couldn't put this off forever. "All right, I'll take it."

"Mr. Sloan, this is Jonathan Gumby."

"Yes, Mr. Gumby. I read your article in this morning's paper." Zach knew his tone could have melted glass so he struggled to control it.

"We'd like to hear your side, to be fair."

Fair? what a joke! The press was ready to crucify him. The image of the dead woman assaulted him before he could dodge it. Did he deserve the media's scorn?

"I'll give a statement, Gumby, but only if you swear to print all of it, not a few selected bits."

"Okay. When?"

"Can you be here in ten minutes?"

"Yes."

Zach hung up and looked at the papers his lawyer had faxed him. Spence Campbell had helped him draft a statement that morning. On Spence's advice, Zach had waited until the press contacted him even though his instinct was to defend himself immediately against the newspaper attack. Being too defensive would make him look guilty, Spence had said.

Guilty. Was he? He'd gone over the specs so many times he could recite them by rote. No, something else was responsible for the collapse.

The foundation? He'd overseen most of the excavation. Not all. He'd been served with divorce papers in the midst of the digging and had spent a couple of afternoons with Spence analyzing his options.

First, he'd tried to fight the separation. Later, when he realized Annie was going ahead with it no matter what he did, he'd wanted a settlement that was fair to her. It had ticked him off royally that she wouldn't accept any money for their shared assets. He'd ended up putting it in investments for her. He'd bet the money was still there today. Annie had vowed she'd never touch it.

In the end, he'd lost Annie anyway—and maybe a lot more. What had he missed by not being there when the building crew did the test pits? When they put in the footings?

"YOU'RE CRAZY, you know that?"

At least she was laughing. And her color was better. Her freckled cheeks were pink with amusement.

"Why is that?" he asked, answering her grin.

Annie picked up a book. "Zach, we only need one or two of these."

He glanced at the pile. "They're all different. Look at the titles."

Sitting back on her couch, Daisy at her feet, he watched her shuffle through the fourteen books he'd bought on childbirth, pregnancy and child rearing. The salesclerk had also thought he was nuts.

"Talk To Your Baby?" Annie asked.

"Ah, that's my favorite. I had a chance to skim it when I grabbed something to eat at the mall."

Annie's eyes danced. "And?"

"Well, it says babies can hear in the womb."

"I know that. Not until later, though."

"That's just speculation. Anyway, you should play good music for them. And if you play an instrument, they can feel the vibrations."

"Zach, that's nothing new."

"I know. But this book goes further." He took it from her, opened to an earmarked page and read aloud, "One of the newest theories of innovative researchers is the concept of talking to your baby. Telling it things about the world, about you, about your values and what you believe in."

Annie shook her head. "That sounds straight from Sonya's books on mysticism."

He continued to read. "Most people initially balk at this idea." He gave her a superior grin. "But obstetricians say that even if the baby can't internalize what's said, the sound of the parents' voices is soothing. It particularly gives fathers a chance to bond."

She rolled her eyes.

"And," he read further, "parents get to verbalize things they may not have told each other, things they've never even articulated to themselves."

Annie's smile faded.

"What is it, honey?"

"In the past, sometimes I felt...I felt there were times when neither of us really knew what the other was thinking. That we jumped to too many conclusions about each other."

He hesitated, but finally he admitted, "I think you're right. I...um, I always had such a hard time revealing my inner thoughts, my fears. There was nobody there to listen when I was a kid, so I just got used to keeping everything to myself.''

She nodded sympathetically.

"So, how about it?" He lightened his tone. "Shall we talk to the baby?"

"I don't know. It sounds pretty far-fetched to me."

"Come here."

With only a slight hesitation, she slid closer on the couch.

"Put your feet up. Relax. Close your eyes."

"Why?"

"The book says to."

"Maybe we should dim the lights and get some of Sonya's incense."

"Hush, just do it. I'll close mine, too."

When she was settled, he placed his hand right over her womb, where his tiny child rested. One book had said the baby was no bigger than the tip of his little finger and looked like a fish.

"I'll go first," he said.

"You're damn right you will."

"Shh, no swearing in front of our baby."

He felt her chuckle.

Leaning back, too, he rubbed his left hand in a slow circle on her belly.

Annie sighed. "Mmm."

"Hi, baby, this is your daddy. I gotta tell you, I feel dumb doing this, but...but I want you to know me before you come out, so I'm giving it a try. If you think it's crazy, then blame me. Not your mother. It's all my idea, and she thinks it's crazy.''

He was silent a minute, wondering where to begin. ''The first thing you need to know is how much I want you. Someday, you might overhear that I didn't want kids.'' Zach took a deep breath. ''Well, I didn't. I took care of my younger brothers and sisters for ten years, and I'd had my fill. My uncle got me out of all that, and I thought for a long time, his was the kind of life I wanted. But sweetheart, I don't feel that way now. I want you more than I've ever wanted anything in my life.'' He drew in a breath, and the rest just slipped out. ''Except for your mother and me to be together again.''

He felt Annie tense. God, he hoped he hadn't blown it by revealing too much.

''Anyway, just know that you've been wanted right from the beginning, even if you were a bit of a surprise.'' His voice caught at the end, strangled by the force of his emotions.

Annie's small, warm hand covered his in silent support. After a moment, she began softly, ''Hi, honey, this is your mommy. I do think this is kind of crazy, but it's a good crazy.'' She giggled a little nervously. ''I want you, too, very much. I've always wanted you, right from the minute I met your daddy.'' She hesitated, then squeezed Zach's hand. ''I never, ever stopped wanting his baby,'' she whispered.

Zach's throat clogged and he turned his hand so their fingers laced. *Thank you, God.*

"Yeah, sweetheart," Annie said. "I want you so much, I even went to see a doctor today."

Zach bolted upright and his eyes flew open. "Annie..."

"Zachary Sloan, you're cheating. Sit back and close those baby blues."

As he settled back, his fingers tightened on hers. "You see," she continued, "I can be stubborn, sometimes. But I know I can't afford to take any chances with you, so I went to see this big-time doctor. Dr. Barry was very nice. He told me my midwife has a good reputation. He said to trust her."

"Okay, we will," Zach said, surprising Annie. "But I'd really hoped Dr. Barry could help with the morning sickness."

Eyes still closed, Annie said, "Actually, he did. He said he'd always believed that cravings a woman has during pregnancy are significant. Instead of being folklore, he thinks that women crave foods that settle their stomachs. He told me to give it a try."

"Has it helped?" Zach asked.

"Hey, is this a conversation with my baby or you?" she teased.

He laughed. "Okay, okay, tell the baby."

"Yes, it helped," Annie said haughtily. "A little bit. I've been wanting vanilla milk shakes. I made one and I felt better after drinking it."

Zach's hmmph was smug.

"But your daddy shouldn't be so smug about this. Your grandma also talked me into going to see a Chinese masseuse who's had success in curing morning sickness."

Laughter erupted out of Zach. It was deep, from his belly.

And it brought tears to Annie's eyes. She'd missed that laugh, the one she'd heard as he told her silly jokes in the middle of the night when she couldn't sleep. The one she'd heard when she tried to play football with him and he'd tackle her and call her a sissy—so she'd tickle him and he'd laugh and laugh. It was also the one she hadn't heard the last several months of their marriage.

We lost so much.

Trying to ease the sadness, she said, "Oh, tell your daddy not to laugh. Daddies are encouraged to come to the massage sessions, too. Apparently, he needs to learn some of the techniques, to help us through this."

"Hmm…" she heard Zach say. "I'll have to give Mommy massages? This pregnancy is getting to be more and more interesting every day, sweetheart. More and more interesting."

CHAPTER FOUR

ANNIE HAD BEEN RIGHT about a lot of things, Zach reflected, not the least of which was her assessment of the person sitting across from him. Martin Mann was one of the most successful builders in the Boston area. He was also a cocky, self-serving son of a bitch. Zach wondered why he'd ever cultivated the man's friendship.

"So, how are you holding up, Sloan?" Mann asked, lazing back in a chair. He crossed his ankle over a knee, revealing Italian-leather shoes. To complement his Armani suit. Once Zach would have been impressed by the expensive clothes. But no more.

Forcing his jaw to relax, Zach said, "I'm fine. And you? How are you holding up?"

Only a slight arch of his eyebrow revealed that Mann recognized the innuendo. "Well, you have more to lose than I do at this point."

Zach steepled his hands and gave Mann one of his best glacial stares. "Do I? Why is that, Martin?"

"Because OSHA decided to start with investigating the beams."

"Ah, yes, the beams. The ones you asked to have

changed. I always wondered why you submitted such a low bid and then requested a change order right away.''

Mann's laugh was silky. ''Happens all the time, Zach. Once I got into it, I thought we might need more support in the foundation.''

A knock on the door cut off Zach's reply. ''Come in.''

Les Corrigan entered the office. He was red-faced, a little out of breath—and something else Zach couldn't put his finger on. ''Sorry I'm late. Traffic...then my son—'' He stopped abruptly. ''Aw, hell, you don't wanna know all that, Zach.'' He extended his arm for a warm handshake, then plunked his large frame into a chair and looked at Mann and smiled weakly. ''Martin.''

''Les.''

''Thanks for coming, Les. I appreciate it,'' Zach said.

''So, where do we start?'' Was there an edge in Mann's voice? The builder had resisted this meeting. When he'd realized Zach wouldn't budge, Mann had asked to have it at his own offices. Home-court advantage, Zach knew, and had insisted they come to him.

''I'd like to go over some of the specs with you two.'' Zach tapped his pen on a thick manila folder filled with computer printouts. ''Since I'm certain OSHA won't find that an insufficiency in the beams caused the collapse, I'd like to review some other

aspects of the structure.'' He handed both men fold-
ers containing test-pit logs, submittals of bolt testing,
welding reports, steel-mill certificates and other rel-
evant data. He waited until they opened the files.

"Where do we start?'' Mann asked again, after
perusing the contents.

"Let's start at the beginning of my checklist,''
Zach suggested.

"The slope was all right—a forty-five-degree angle,'' Mann said, looking at the printouts. "It took a
minimum of excavation.''

"I agree,'' Corrigan put in.

Zach crossed off the first notation. "I was there
that day. Seemed to go well.''

They discussed a few more easily eliminated fac-
tors.

"Let's spend some time on the test pits.''

"Sure,'' Mann said.

Corrigan said nothing.

"You did twelve, right?''

"That's what the grid says.''

"It was four-thousand-pound bearing capacity,
right?''

"Yes.''

"And the soil analysis held up?''

"Of course.''

"Is that the usual number of pits you do?''

Mann looked at him. "It's standard for this size
building. Why?''

"I'd like to have a better handle on the foundation."

The contractor eyed him carefully. "That's right, you weren't there during all the digging, were you? Something about your wife?"

I was with my lawyer trying to hang on to my marriage. "That's right."

"I remember now," Mann continued. "Annie divorced you while the building was going up."

"This investigation must be hard for you, Zach." Corrigan's frown was sincere. "It must bring up a lot of memories."

Another irony. Zach could still see Marion Corrigan's strained face when she came to see him, begging him to give Les a chance at the museum. He needed it, she'd said. Their marriage needed it. And because Zach's own marital problems were on the rise, he'd sympathized and picked his old fraternity brother, who'd just established his own firm, to be the structural engineer.

Had he been a fool?

Annie hadn't thought so...

Zach, it could make a real difference in his business.

But it would make more sense to go with a more established engineering firm.

Les and Marion need this, Zach...

Who would have guessed the Corrigans would have paid back the gesture by helping Zach through his messy divorce? But in the end, their own marriage had gotten rockier, and they broke up a year or two year later. Zach had been glad when Les told him they'd reconciled.

"Zach?"

Les's voice brought him out of his reverie. "No, Les, the investigation isn't as hard for me as you might think," Zach said, smiling at the image of Annie. Pregnant. With *his* baby. "As you know, Annie was there the night the staircase collapsed. We've...been seeing each other again."

"Don't blame you, Sloan." Mann smiled lasciviously. "She's still got the nicest ass in town."

Zach bolted out of his seat. "You're talking about my wife, Mann."

"Ex-wife," Mann said archly.

"Just watch what you say about her."

Corrigan intervened. "Let's get back to the museum."

Zach controlled himself by sinking back down and rereading part of the report. Finally he asked, "So the soil was packed enough. Right?"

"Absolutely."

"You didn't need to bring in any topsoil at all?"

"None," Mann said.

"Lucky for you, Martin. It would have cost you thousands." After the job was bid, the standard contract read that any additional improvements of the land were at the builder's expense. That kind of error would have cost Mann dearly, which was why Zach believed the builder would have paid particular attention to that detail.

"Yeah, lucky."

Zach turned to Les. "Was there a test pit done on the exact spot where the beam for the staircase is anchored?"

Les shuffled the papers. "Ah, let me see."

"Page three. The grid shows there was," Mann said smoothly.

"That's right." Zach knew the answer. He'd checked and rechecked every item. But he wanted to see the other men's reactions. Documentation could be altered. "Let's go to the stats on the concrete and steel, then. I'd like to revisit the concrete pourings."

Mann slapped the folder on his knee. "Are you implying something was wrong with them?"

Leaning over on his elbows, Zach faced down the builder. He noticed sweat had beaded on Mann's upper lip. "I don't know, Martin. The pouring canisters check out. But are you sure there were no honeycombs in the actual laying of the foundation?"

"I'm sure."

Zach looked at Corrigan. "Les?"

"I was there, too. It was poured right."

"Well, something went wrong," Zach answered. "And I'll tear apart every statistic here until I find it. I'm convinced the error wasn't my design."

"And it wasn't my foundation," Mann said.

"Time will tell, I guess."

Mann glared at Zach.

Zach looked over at Corrigan. Les shrugged and gave him a weak grin.

ANNIE STARED at the computer screen in her den, willing her stomach to settle down. For some reason, the blinking cursor made her even more queasy, and she'd made little progress on her thesis. Nibbling on crackers and drinking half a vanilla milk shake helped, but she still felt shaky.

For the tenth time, she glanced at the clock. Only seven-thirty at night and she was dead tired already. Returning to work had drained her energy. Yawning, she'd given up trying to focus, when the doorbell rang. Daisy barked expectantly.

Easing from the chair, Annie made her way to the front of the house hoping it was Zach. For the last two weeks, he'd stopped over every night to check on her, brought dinner or sometimes a video, and always spent time talking to the baby. Annie chuckled. He was really being a sap over this pregnancy.

She swung open the door, smile in place. But instead of her ex-husband, she found Peter Jenkins.

"Peter."

"Hi, love." He took her in his arms.

Annie shivered.

"It's so good to see you," he said.

When he buried his face in her neck, she stiffened and turned her head away. She couldn't let him kiss her.

"Honey, what's wrong?" Peter pulled back and cradled her face in his hands. "Surprised?"

"Very."

He hugged her again, then stepped away. Bending down, he tried to pat Daisy's head. The dog barked at him, then darted into the kitchen.

Peter shook his head. "I see absence hasn't made Daisy any fonder of me."

"I told you before, she probably senses you're allergic to her."

"We'll work that out, Annie."

The innocence of that statement doubled her guilt. There was a lot more wrong than Daisy.

Though he was smiling, Peter's eyes were wary. Annie thought about what a good man he was, how he'd always given her the space she'd needed... *I can wait for the sex, Annie, until you're ready... Of course I want to move in, but I can see now's not the time... I'll be gone a while, we'll talk about marriage when I get back...*

Usually, she found his utter unselfishness admirable. Today, it added to her guilt. Shaking off the thought, Annie stepped aside for him to enter. In the living room, she folded her arms across her chest, hoping to ease the ache there. "When did you get in?"

"About an hour ago. I took a cab here right from the airport."

Closing her eyes briefly, she was horrified at the thought that he might have come to her house and found Zach there. Peter deserved much better than that.

Annie felt a wave of guilt. Peter didn't know she was pregnant with Zach's child. She hadn't wanted to break the news over the phone, but she should have written. She'd planned to do that, but the words had been difficult to find, and she'd put it off. Now it was too late.

"Let's sit, Annie." Tugging her down to the couch, Peter clasped her hand.

Gently he rubbed his thumb underneath her eye. "You look exhausted. Tough few weeks?"

"Yes."

"I read about the collapse of the Pierce Museum's staircase."

"The press is like a dog with a bone."

"There was a casualty, wasn't there?"

She nodded. "It was awful."

He examined her face. She willed herself not to flinch. "It was Sloan's building," he said softly.

"Yes, it was."

"I hope the bastard didn't screw this up, like he did everything else."

Bleak blue eyes flashed into Annie's mind. "So do I."

"Did you see him?"

"Yes. He helped secure the building so the rescue work could take place."

"Was it tough?"

Annie drew in a steadying breath. "Peter, I spent some time with Zach that night."

Pulling back, Peter asked, "How much time?"

Annie didn't answer, but a blush crept up her neck to her face.

Peter was heartbreakingly quiet for several seconds. "I see." He tried for a smile. "Guess this wasn't the best time to leave you alone for twelve weeks, was it?"

She covered his hand with hers. "It wasn't that."

"No, I know it wasn't. You've been in love with him all this time. I've always dreaded your seeing him again."

"You never told me that."

"I didn't want to upset you."

"We should have talked about your feelings."

"My feelings don't matter now. What does matter is how much he hurt you. Don't do anything rash."

I already did.

She was surprised when he pulled her into his arms again. "I'm your friend, as well as being in love with you, Annie. Let's talk this out."

"It's too late for that." Drawing back, she raised her hand to his face. "I'm pregnant, Peter. It happened that night."

Hurt clouded Peter's warm brown eyes. He stood and walked to the window. She let him go, wishing she could help alleviate the pain she'd caused, but knowing she couldn't.

After several long seconds, he turned around.

"You aren't going back to him, are you? Not after what he did to you?"

"I don't know what I'm going to do. He wants to be part of raising the child."

Peter's expression was indignant. "He never wanted any kids."

"No, he didn't. But he's changed. He wants to be part of the baby's life. I think he has that right."

"To the child. Not to you."

"No, not to me."

Quickly, Peter crossed to her and sank back down on the couch. "Marry me, Annie. I'll take care of you both."

Annie was flabbergasted. Surely what he was suggesting transcended what was...normal. Immediately she scolded herself for the unkind thought. "No, Peter, it wouldn't be right."

"I'd never treat you or the child badly."

Moved, she squeezed his arm. "I know you wouldn't. It's just that I..." She couldn't finish.

"You want *him.*"

"I don't know what I want."

"I see." He edged away from her and glanced around the room. "Well, this is going to take some getting used to."

They'd been together for two years. It would be hard for him. And for her, too, Annie realized. Tears welled in her eyes but she fought them. The last thing Peter needed was to have to comfort her.

"I guess I'll leave now."

"You can stay for a while," she offered.

"No, no, I need some time…"

"All right."

They both rose. She walked with him to the door. After he opened it, he faced her and hugged her tightly. When he drew away, she felt her stomach roil again. His eyes were wet.

"I'll call you. To see how you are. To see how things work out."

"Okay. Peter…I'm sor—"

"Shh…don't say anything. I don't want your pity. I wanted your love."

He hurried away from her and down the stairs. Annie closed the door before he could see her cry. Stumbling to the couch, she dropped onto it. The full flood of tears came then, and she cried hard for a man she'd hurt…a man who deserved so much better. Daisy wandered in and tried to nuzzle her, but Annie resisted the dog. When the doorbell rang less than a minute later, Annie wiped her face and went to answer it, Daisy tagging along.

Zach stood at the doorway, hands in his pockets, his blue eyes blazing. They narrowed on her, and she saw the exact moment he realized she'd been crying. His jaw tensed. Absently, he rubbed Daisy's head, but kept his eyes on Annie. "I take it that was Peter."

She nodded.

"I was pulling into the driveway…I saw him hold

you." In contrast to the passion in his eyes, Zach's voice was deadly cold.

Without saying more, he brushed past her and strode into the living room, the dog following. There, he paced and plowed his hand through his hair. Fatigue got the better of Annie and she followed him in and sank onto the chair. Finally, Zach turned to face her. "Did you tell him about the baby?"

"Yes."

"And?"

"And what, Zach? He was shocked and hurt."

"What did he say?"

"He asked me to marry him."

"What?"

Annie bit her tongue. The revelation just slipped past her already battered defenses. She leaned back onto the pillows and closed her eyes. "I'm sorry, I shouldn't have told you that."

When he didn't answer, she opened her eyes and saw that he had frozen midstride.

"What answer did you give him?" Zach asked.

"I said no, of course."

"Why?"

"I can't marry one man when I'm—"

He pounced on her clipped comment. "When you're what?"

"Nothing."

"You're what, Annie?"

"When I'm carrying another man's child."

"That wasn't what you were going to say."

"Yes, it was."

"You're so stubborn, you can't even admit—"

"Listen, Zach, I don't have time for this. I was busy before Peter came. I've got to have my thesis done by the end of the month, and I'm not finished typing it yet."

"What thesis?"

"For my Ph.D. from Boston University in social work."

"I didn't know you were getting your doctorate."

She raised her chin. "There's a lot you don't know about me."

"Well, one thing I do know is that you're exhausted. You don't have the stamina to work on a doctorate and hold down a full-time job. You'll have to give up the thesis temporarily."

"There you go again. Who gave you the right to tell me what I can or can't do?"

"I have rights by virtue of that child you're carrying. Somebody's got to watch out for you when you insist on being foolish with your energy."

"I am *not* giving up my thesis. I'll have my doctorate this fall, and I'm thinking about going into private practice as a therapist in a year or two. I won't let you alter my plans." She drew in a deep breath to help banish the queasiness their confrontation had caused.

Zach stared at her. Then his shoulders sagged. Annie remembered he'd had a meeting with the contractor and engineer and wondered what news he'd gotten today.

"I'm sorry," he finally said. "I'm not helping, am I? By busting in here and acting like a caveman."

"You're actually apologizing for your bullying? That's new."

He came closer and knelt in front of her. Threading his hand in her hair, he sieved it through his fingers. His eyes darkened with another kind of emotion. Leaning over, he placed his lips gently on her forehead. Then he kissed her nose. "I've changed, sweetheart. Give me the chance to show you. *We* can get mar—"

He broke off at the sound of the doorbell.

Weary, Annie sighed and Daisy barked again. Had Peter come back? She didn't think she could take a scene with him and Zach. Then she heard from the foyer, "Annie? Are you home?"

Annie stiffened. Just before Zach did. They both recognized the voice of Lucy…Zach's sister.

When Lucy appeared in the doorway to the living room, Zach was still kneeling at Annie's feet, though he pulled away and stood quickly.

"Oh my God," Lucy said. Her tall frame tensed, and her eyes—the exact blue of Zach's—narrowed on him. "What the hell are you doing here?" She looked down at Annie. "Are you all right?"

"Of course I am." The strain between brother and sister was acute, and Annie knew what was coming.

She'd played referee between them more times than she could count.

"What's he doing here?" Lucy repeated.

Zach said, "Lucy, listen, I know you—"

"You don't know anything, Zach. Keep out of this."

In a supreme effort to control himself, he turned his back on his sister and walked to the window. His shoulders were stiff, and Annie suspected the words had cut deeply.

"Sit down, Lucy," she said.

"Annie—"

"Sit down. I've got something to tell you."

"All I want to know is what that bastard is doing in your house. After what he did to you..."

Zach turned then. "And what did I do to *you* that's made you hate me so much?"

Lucy's temper triggered as easily as Zach's. "What did you do to me?" She stomped closer and faced him squarely. "You rejected me when you were a teenager and never bothered with me as an adult. You rejected every member of our family to become some hotshot in town. Then you rejected Annie when you hit the fast track. Three strikes and you're out, brother dear."

Zach blanched when she finished, but said nothing. Fleetingly, Annie wondered how he was going to withstand this newest blow amidst all the other things that had happened to him in the last few weeks.

"Stop it, Lucy. Right now. I won't let you treat

your brother that way. I've told you for years your grudge against him was unreasonable. Now listen to what I have to say."

"Nothing you could say could make me change my mind about him."

"Not even that you're going to be an aunt?"

Lucy's jaw gaped. "An aunt?" Her eyes dropped to Annie's stomach. "An *aunt?*"

"I'm pregnant."

"Pregnant?"

She stared at Annie, then turned to Zach. Without warning, she raised her hand and slapped him across the face. Zach jerked back, but again he said nothing.

Horrified, Annie circled the couch and crossed to them. She grabbed Lucy's wrist and held on tight. "That's enough, Lucy. I'm as much responsible for this baby as he is. Stop this tirade now, or I'll have to ask you to leave my house."

Lucy deflated visibly. Tears welled in her eyes. "Why, Annie, why? You don't love him anymore. He's been horrible to all of us."

Annie cleared her throat. Zach was staring at her and she felt as if she was on some kind of precipice. He was waiting for her to say she loved him.

She looked from one pair of eyes to the other—both a deep deep blue, both filled with pain.

Waiting for her response.

WHY WAS HE HERE? Zach asked himself the next day as he pulled open the door to the old building that

housed Lansing's social services. He scanned the
arched windows and Palladian facade. He'd always
admired how the stone accented the structure's
height, but gave it warmth, too. And the place had
sentimental value. This was the building where Annie had worked when they were married. She'd left
to go to the Red Cross and now she'd come back
here. Full circle, he thought ruefully.

She hadn't come full circle personally, though, ev-
idenced by the fact that last night she hadn't said she
loved him. She wouldn't say it. For the first time
since the collapse of the staircase, Zach wondered if
he could take the pain of trying to win Annie back.

He found Annie's floor and while waiting in line
until the receptionist was free, he thought about
Lucy. He'd left soon after Annie's revelation so she
could talk to his sister privately. Again, he felt the
jab of Lucy's wrath. Knowing he deserved her scorn
only made him feel worse. When he'd left home for
college, he'd cut himself off from his family for
years, trying to find his own sense of self. When he
married Annie, he'd gotten back into the fold somewhat, but then when they divorced, he'd been uncomfortable again around his family. Though he still
visited them, things were strained, particularly with
his father and Lucy.

Frustrated, Zach shifted his thoughts to work, always his safety valve. But not today. They'd lost a
job, and Devon was disappointed because it had been
one that he'd brought in. And a big one, at that.

Again, one of Gumby's articles had been in the paper. A special feature, it focused on several cities around the country where an elaborate and unusual design had caused problems. The firm Devon had courted alluded to the paper when they'd decided to go with a more traditional architect. Sloan Associates would suffer financially until the cause of the collapse was found. Forcibly Zach stifled the panic that welled inside him as he wondered once again if he was at fault.

"May I help you?" The young woman behind the desk eyed him appreciatively. She hadn't been here when he and Annie were married, so she didn't recognize him.

"I'd like to see Annie Montgomery."

The receptionist arched an eyebrow. "Annie?" Taking in his suit and tie, she added, "May I ask who wants to see her?"

"Zachary Sloan."

"Annie's ex?"

Small offices, Zach thought. He wondered if they knew yet that she was pregnant.

"Yes. She's still here, isn't she?"

"Yeah." The young woman continued staring. "But she's not in her office. She went into the back room to—"

"Zach, what are you doing here?"

Pivoting, he saw Annie framed in the old oak archway. Her hair was braided and stuffed up under a red baseball cap. To match the red T-shirt she wore.

Over snug denim cutoffs. The long expanse of leg that tucked into sneakers made his mouth water. "Going out for the Red Sox?" he teased.

She smiled and he sucked in his breath as he remembered other smiles.

"Not the Red Sox exactly. What are you doing here? Did you get my messages?"

"Yes, did you get mine?"

"Uh-huh. Sorry we missed each other." She studied his face. "Bad day?"

"Yeah, kind of."

The receptionist watched them as if she was glued to a soap opera.

"I'd love to talk, but I've got to be at the field by seven." Annie touched her stomach. "And I've got to eat."

"The field?"

Grabbing his arm, she said, "Come on, walk with me to the diner." She held on to him as they left her floor. Her breasts, which he'd noticed stretched the cotton of the T-shirt visibly, were already fuller with her pregnancy. They brushed his biceps. Contact with them made his body tighten and he yanked his suit coat together.

"Where are you going?" he asked as they made their way out of the building and crossed the street to a place called Mickey's. She halted out in front.

"Part of my new job is working with a downtown youth group. I drew the ten-year-olds. Boys."

He scanned her outfit. "You're going to play ball with them?"

"Actually, I'm going to coach their summer baseball team."

"You?"

She giggled. "Yeah, funny, isn't it?"

"Annie, you don't know anything about the game."

"Are you kidding? I watched you play baseball your whole senior year. And I was at every one of your softball games when we were married."

Zach remembered. Her yelling like a banshee from the stands. The huge hugs and kisses when he starred in a game. The long, lazy back rubs, which eventually led to great sex.

"Yeah," he said hoarsely. "I remember."

Annie blushed. Turning away fast—he guessed to hide her reaction—she swayed and clutched the doorframe. "Oh."

He caught her arm. "Are you all right?"

"Yeah. I just can't move that fast without getting dizzy."

"Oh, fine. How are you going to keep up with nine ten-year-olds on a baseball diamond?"

"I'll manage." When she faced him, she'd turned white again.

"Come on, let's go inside. Get you something to eat." Her face paled even more. "A vanilla milk shake, remember?"

She gave him a weak smile and leaned on his arm. Her fragility unnerved him.

After they were seated, and she'd nibbled on a grilled-cheese sandwich and sipped a milk shake, he said, "Honey, you can't do this."

Her eyes narrowed. "Please, Zach, don't start. It seems that's all you're telling me these days—just like before."

Trying to heed her warning, he gentled his tone. "I want to watch out for you now."

"I've taken care of myself for almost six years. I don't need you to do it anymore."

Her stubbornness triggered his temper—as always. "I've done it since you were eighteen, Annie," he said, not hiding the exasperation in his voice. "Cut me some slack. It's a hard habit to break."

Her eyes softened. "And you took care of your brothers and sisters for years before that."

He rubbed his cheek where Lucy had hit him. "Yeah. I did a great job with them, didn't I?"

Annie reached over and covered his other hand. "She'll come around, Zach. But you have to reach out to her, to all of them. You have to meet them halfway."

Ah, the perennial advice. How many times had she told him the same thing in their life together... *We're going to your parents' for dinner, Zach... Your father means well, he's just reacting to your neglect... Your uncle Cary was good for you, but your family feels bad...like you chose him over them.*

Zach had! At eighteen, he'd have been crazy not to escape the dilapidated house that could never meet the needs of ten people, to find refuge in his uncle's pricey condo and country club.

"I don't want to talk about my family," Zach said.

Annie looked as if she might argue, but sat back against the vinyl instead. "Well, you'll have to think about them soon. I plan to tell the rest of your family about the baby on Sunday."

"Sunday?"

"At dinner. I still go. As often as I can. Sometimes they invite my mother, too."

"I didn't know." Probably because he'd avoided Sunday dinner. It was a painful reminder of Annie.

"They talk about you, you know."

"Oh, I'll bet."

"Martha shows me every single birthday and Mother's Day gift you send. She's particularly fond of the gold locket. She has your picture in it."

Zach smiled at the image of his mother carrying the sixtieth birthday present he'd given her close to her heart.

"She'd rather see you, though, Zach."

"I visit."

"Rarely. And only when your dad's not there."

"At his request."

"Your mother says he looks at your scrapbooks all the time."

Pain—unexpected in its intensity—almost made him groan aloud. He hadn't know that, either.

"Do you want to come with me to tell them?"

"They'll have a fit."

"Maybe. Maybe not."

He snorted.

"I'd like you to be there. If you could come for dinner, it would mean a lot to them. And to me."

"I don't know, Annie."

"Well, think about it." She glanced at her watch. "I've got to go."

"Where's your car?"

"Over at the office. But I'm walking the two blocks to the field."

"Alone?"

She gave him a scathing look and stood.

He followed her out of the restaurant. When he began to walk with her, she frowned.

"Humor me, okay?" he told her. "Let me walk with you at least."

"All right."

As they trekked down the street, he asked, "How did you end up coaching this team? It can't be in your job description."

She chuckled. "No, the coach and sponsor backed out at the last minute."

"Do you *want* to do this?"

"Well, I didn't mind before I got pregnant." She swallowed hard. "It's going to be a stretch now." She smiled. "I'll be all right, but we're still scrambling for a sponsor."

"Who sponsors the teams?"

"Local businesses."

"Have I ever been asked?"

"I don't know."

They walked farther before Zach said, "Sloan Associates will sponsor your team."

Stopping midstride, she stared at him. "Really? That's great. You have to buy T-shirts and put up a nominal fee." She scowled, but her face was full of color and animation. "I hope the kids have gloves and balls." She tugged on the oversize bag she carried. "I have a few extra things in here..."

"I'll buy the equipment," Zach said gruffly, embarrassed by the fact that the cost of one pair of his shoes could probably provide the team with all the gloves and balls they needed.

She touched his shoulder. "Thanks, Zach. It means a lot to me."

Without considering his action, he leaned over and kissed her. On the mouth. Just a slight, wispy brush of his lips. She grasped his arms, steadying herself. And she moaned. The sound sent a jolt of desire through him.

Struggling to remember they were on a street in downtown Lansing, he drew back and stared at her, then took her hand and laced his fingers with hers. They walked the rest of the way to the field with their hands linked, talking about the team.

Once there, a swarm of boys surrounded Annie, edging him to the outside of their group.

"She's here," the first little kid yelled.

"I told ya she'd come."

"So what? She's a girl. We ain't never had a girl coach."

Annie laughed and ruffled heads of hair and tugged on a few caps. Though they were complaining, most of them looked at her with gratitude.

Zach's amusement fled when she bent to reach in her bag. Suddenly, she went pale and swayed again. Righting herself, she closed her eyes to regain her equilibrium.

He threaded his way to her through the kids. "Annie, sit down." Gently prodding her onto a wooden bench, he left his hands on her shoulders.

A wide-eyed boy asked, "She sick?"

"Who're you?" another wanted to know.

Zach looked down at the faces peering up at him. One of them had eyes just like his brother Ben's. Zach remembered teaching Ben, Frank and Kent to hit and field a ball. Nostalgia washed over him. Mostly, his childhood memories were of a time fraught with adolescent rebellion. He didn't often remember the good ones.

"This is Zach," Annie said. "He's offered to sponsor your team."

Yelps went up from the boys, making Zach wince.

"Least we got that, even if we got a girl coach who don't know nothin' about baseball."

Zach bit his lip to keep from laughing.

"Hey, guys, I'm the best you got," Annie told them.

"You sure you ain't sick?"

She was. Zach could see the fatigue that came over her every night about this time. And he'd bet her stomach was churning. She could never run around on the field in the heat of a June evening. He'd be damned if he'd let her.

Stepping away, he shrugged out of his suit coat and tossed it on the bench. His tie joined it. As he rolled up his cuffs, he said, "Hey, you guys, ever hear of the MIT Beavers?"

One little boy said, "Yeah, I saw their picture in the paper at the store where I shine shoes."

"I used to play on that team," Zach told them, lifting a bat and taking a practice swing. It felt…right. He hadn't held one since Annie left him and he'd quit the softball league to concentrate on being the best architect in town.

"So?" one kid asked warily.

"How'd you like a former pitcher for the Beavers as a coach?"

"What was your record?"

"My last year, I had seventeen wins, two losses."

"How about your batting average?"

"Six hundred."

Several kids gave a low whistle.

Zach caught Annie's gaze over their heads. She had tears in her eyes.

"Hey, Annie, don't cry," one boy said, tracking Zach's stare. "You can be our assistant, can't she, mister?"

"Sure she can," Zach said, fighting the hoarseness in his voice caused by the soft approval on her face. "This okay?" he asked, holding up the bat. "I don't mean to take over again. It's just that you're so sick…"

Annie glanced from Zach to the boys. She placed her hand over her stomach. "Yeah, it's okay. Baby and I will sit this season out, I guess." Then she took in a deep breath and glared at Zach with faked sternness. "Just don't get used to this kind of easy surrender, Sloan."

Zach smiled. Inside, he admitted he'd take *any* kind of surrender from her. Any time.

CHAPTER FIVE

NEXT TO THE Pierce Museum, Jackson Gage's house was Zach's favorite design. It rose out of the ground, four stories of wood and glass and brick, with a full wall of windows, top to bottom, facing south. As Zach sat on the flagstone patio the Sunday afternoon following his baseball endeavor, sipping coffee and gazing out at the five wooded acres, tennis court, golf tee and ponds, he remembered how he'd gotten this project. Gage had been a member of the board of directors for the Pierce Museum, and had asked Zach to design his house just weeks after the museum project was completed. Zach hadn't done residential structures in a while, but he'd consented to this request as a favor to the older man.

Though Gage hadn't indicated what he wanted when he'd issued the invitation here today, Zach was hoping to secure the design for Gage's new electronics plant. One of the things Annie had always hated about his job was that as much business transpired on weekends on golf courses as on weekdays in the office.

"Sorry to keep you waiting, son," Gage said as

he joined Zach on the deck. "You'd think all of those bankers would be out playing golf on Sunday."

"Surprised you aren't, Jack."

"Got carpal tunnel," the older man said, holding up his chunky wrists. "It's hell getting old."

"You'll never be old."

"Celebrating my seventieth birthday in a couple of months."

"Yes, I know."

"You're gonna make the to-do at the club, aren't you?"

"Wouldn't miss it for the world. They're combining it with your Citizen of the Year Award, aren't they?"

Gage waved off the accolade. "You're a good friend, Zach." He scowled. "That's why I asked you here today. I've got to make decisions about the plant by Thanksgiving."

Zach willed himself to relax, but his nerves felt like guitar strings drawn too tightly. If Jackson Gage passed him by for the new project, Lansing's building community would think Zach was at fault for the collapse of the museum. "I know you do." Zach held the other man's gaze. "I hope you're still considering me."

"One thing I always liked about you, Zach, was your straightforwardness." Gage sighed. "I'll be candid. I've been advised to bypass you."

"By?"

"Can't tell you that. This Pierce thing doesn't look good."

"I know." Zach set down his coffee. "But I'm convinced I'll be exonerated." *Except in my nightmares.* "My design was safe. Something else caused the collapse. The test results on the beams will show they were adequate."

Resting his hands across his midriff, Gage stretched his feet out. He stared at his sprawling lawns thoughtfully. "You work much with Corrigan?"

Surprised at the question, Zach said, "No. After the museum, I left Belton's to start out on my own, and he had all the business he could handle. I hired my own structural engineering staff."

Gage rose and crossed to a flower box brimming with coleus. Bending over, he plucked off a dead shoot. Silhouetted against his house, he looked every bit the successful entrepreneur. Damn, Zach needed his support.

"Rumor has it Corrigan's hit the bottle again," Gage said.

"I'm sorry to hear that. I hope it's not true."

Slowly, the older man faced him. "Any chance he was drinking when he was involved in the Pierce project?"

Zach stood, too. "I don't think so. He'd been going to AA for three years. I believed he was sober when I did the design and for the eighteen months it took to erect the museum. As far as I know, he's still on the wagon. His life seems pretty on track now.''

''But you knew about his problem?''

Zach stuck his hands in his pockets. ''Yes, sir, I did.''

''Not good business sense to use him.''

''People deserve second chances, Jackson.'' Zach thought of his own pleas to Annie. He believed in second chances now more than ever.

Gage stared at him for a long time, then looked back out over the grounds. ''By the time I was thirty, I'd made some money, and the pressure got to me. I started drinking, pretty bad. A good friend got me into Alcoholics Anonymous. The organization saved my life.''

Zach hadn't heard that particular story, but he knew Gage had once had a drinking problem.

''I'm still on the board of directors of the local branch of AA.''

Afraid to hope, Zach watched the older man in silence.

Interminable seconds later, Gage turned to look at him. ''Tell you what I'll do. I'll let it be known you're in the running for the plant. By fall, we might have more news on the museum. If you come out clean, the job's yours.''

Relief washed over Zach. ''I appreciate that, Jackson.''

''I know you do.'' Gage studied him closely.

"Corrigan deserved the second chance you gave him."

"I agree."

"But, if he's drinking again, you should stay away from him professionally, though he could probably use a friend."

Zach suppressed a twinge of regret at no longer being as close as he used to be to Les. He held out his hand. "You won't regret this, Jackson."

Gage's grip was solid. "I hope not." Shrugging off the moment, Gage said, "Now, walk down to the ponds with me. I want to show you my new stock. And I'd like to hear some of your ideas about the plant."

Zach stifled the urge to check his watch and pushed back the guilt. He knew this opportunity to pitch his design was invaluable, even if the job did hinge on what happened with the museum. But he'd agreed to meet Annie at his parents' and he was already late.

"Unless you have to be somewhere," Gage added.

Zach smiled. "Not for a while," he said smoothly. "I'd love to see the ponds. They were my idea, after all."

ANNIE STARED out the window of the Sloans' cramped but homey kitchen, watching the late-afternoon sun set on the maple trees. They'd finished eating, the dishes were done, and she was keeping her mother company while Sonya frosted the dessert she'd brought—all-natural, no-preservatives carrot cake. She'd baked it yesterday after Zach's mother had called to invite her to dinner.

"Not feeling well, dear?" Sonya asked from the counter.

Annie turned. Her mother wore a peasant dress that she'd sewn herself. Her hair was loose and fluffy and made her look young.

"I'm okay now," Annie told her, avoiding the sight of the gooey confection. "Though I was sick before you picked me up to come here."

"When is your appointment with Felicia?"

The Chinese masseuse. "I've had one and I have another at the end of the week. She gave me some really good tips." Annie checked the clock over the sink. She tried to quell her disappointment but was unsuccessful. She'd forgotten what it felt like to wait for Zach. To watch the minutes and hours tick away. To experience the total frustration of his carelessness about his time with her. Or in this case, his time with his family. "He missed dinner. He's not coming at all, I guess."

Sonya said quickly, "Maybe he got tied up."

Frustrated, Annie snapped, "Don't defend him, Mom. He should have come."

Sonya's hand stilled in the act of scooping up another glob of frosting. Finally, she said, "Yes, you're right. He should have."

Before Annie could apologize, Zach's sisters, twelve-year-old Rose and fifteen-year-old Nora, raced into the kitchen, squabbling over a magazine. "He is not the cutest. Annie, what do you think? Is Brad Pitt or Alec Baldwin cuter?"

"What does she know?" David, Zach's college-student brother, teased from the doorway. "She thought Zach was handsome."

"He is," Nora said.

"For a brother," Rose put in.

"Who are we talking about?" Zach's mother, Martha, asked as she joined the group.

"Zach."

Maternal tenderness shone in Martha Sloan's lined face. Seeing that expression made Annie angrier that Zach hadn't come to dinner, that he didn't spend more time with Martha in general. Even today, when Annie planned to tell them about the baby, Zach couldn't make it. Because of work. Just like always.

"Well, are we ready for Sonya's dessert?" Martha asked, indicating the cake.

"I'm not sure I can manage cake," Annie said. "But there's something I want to tell you all. Let's go into the dining room." Against her will, tears clouded Annie's eyes. She loved these people, and had cherished being a part of their family. She glanced at the clock again.

"Annie, are you all right?" Martha came to her side. "You're so flushed."

"I'm a little tired."

Zach's father, John Sloan, was already seated in the dining room when the rest of them entered.

Though they lived nearby, the twins, Lucy and Frank, hadn't made it to dinner, and neither had Ben. But Kent, who was in law school, and David were home for the summer and made an effort to be at Sunday dinner whenever they could. Unlike Zach.

"There you are," John said. He zeroed in on Sonya. "Ah, and dessert."

Sonya brought in the cake and set it on the table. It used to be Annie's favorite, but the sight of it and its sugary smell made her stomach churn. When she got her piece, she cut it into slivers and swished it around the plate. She was waiting to deliver her news until everyone was done so she wouldn't spoil their dessert.

They'll have a fit, Zach had said.

But apparently he wasn't concerned enough to show up for support. Damn him.

The back screen door banged.

"Lucy came, after all?" David wondered aloud.

"Hmmph," John put in, just before Zach appeared in the doorway. His hair windblown, he was dressed in khaki designer shorts and a brown-checked sports shirt and leather Docksiders. He looked cool and sophisticated—and out of place in his childhood home.

Initially no one spoke, the silence was unnerving. Then Kent said, "Well, if it isn't the prodigal son."

"Hush." Zach's mother glared at her fifth child.

David rose, circled the table and clasped Zach's hand. "Good to see you, buddy." The girls shot up and raced to Zach, hugging him warmly. He hugged back, then came to the table to kiss his mother. John Sloan ate his carrot cake in silence.

When everyone reseated themselves, Zach perched on a stool near Martha and caught Annie's gaze. They stared at each other, Annie trying to rein in her disappointment.

Everyone stilled. It took Annie a minute to realize they thought this was the first time she'd seen him since the divorce. She'd asked Lucy not to say anything.

"Hi, Annie," Zach said from across the room.

"Hi."

A chair scraped back. Zach's father stood and faced his oldest son. "Zach."

"Pa."

John turned to the rest of the family. "Excuse me," he said gravely and started for the door.

"Wait, Pa, will you?" At Annie's urgent tone, John halted. "I, um, have something to tell you." She looked around the table. "All of you."

Sonya smiled encouragement, John sat back down and Martha twisted the strings of her apron. The girls watched her with owl eyes.

"I'm pregnant," Annie said bluntly. "I wanted you to know."

It was so quiet Annie could hear the refrigerator humming in the kitchen.

Martha looked at Zach, her expression filled with regret. Slowly she pushed back her chair, stood, went to Annie and hugged her. "Well, this is news. Why didn't you bring Peter, to celebrate with us?"

"Did you and Peter get married?" Rose asked.

Nora leaned over to whisper in Rose's ear.

When Annie chanced a glance at Zach, his features were stony. Very deliberately, he stood and picked his way around the table, between his family members, to stand behind Annie. "It's my baby," he said coolly, settling his hands on her shoulders.

Annie wished she was strong enough to resist his comfort, but the tension in the room was suffocating and it was hard for her to breathe. She leaned into him.

For long seconds, no one spoke. Then Rose said, "That means they—" Nora clapped a hand over her sister's mouth.

Rose shrugged it away. "But they're not married anymore."

Annie waited for Martha or John to deal with the younger children's reaction. John stared down at his cake. Martha looked to Zach. It was startlingly clear that they thought an explanation was *his* responsibility. Annie was struck once more by what life must have been like for Zach growing up in this house.

Squeezing Annie's shoulders, he circled to his sisters, squatted in front of them and took one of each of their hands. "No, girls, we're not married. We should have been more responsible with our actions. We haven't set a very good example for you." Zach glanced up and over at Annie then back to his sisters. "But I love Annie, and I'd like to marry her again."

"Are you gonna?" Nora asked.

"There's a lot to work out first," Zach said.

They gave him accepting grins. Tears leaked from Annie's eyes.

Kent was not so easily won over. "Well, I think it sucks. You don't deserve Annie."

"Watch what you say, young man," Martha said. "If you take Zach's money for law school, you'll show him respect."

Another revelation. Annie hadn't known Zach was paying for Kent's schooling. And probably David's. So much seemed to be *expected* of Zach by this family.

Still somber, John rose and crossed to Annie. He was a quiet, unassuming man who'd always treated her like a daughter. Drawing her into his arms, he hugged her close. Then he left the room. Without a word to Zach.

Silently Zach stood up and stared at his father's back. His lips thinned and his face was set in stern lines. His body was so rigid it hurt Annie to look at him.

Sonya went to Zach and hugged him. He remained stiff for a moment, then returned the embrace.

When Sonya stepped back, Martha crossed to her son for her own hug. "Oh, Zach, our first grandchild."

Zach grasped Martha tightly. Over his mother's

shoulder he looked at Annie. She saw in his eyes all the conflicting emotions that swirled in the room— joy, pain, celebration, old resentments.

And not just between Zach and his family.

ZACH SWUNG HIS CAR into the driveway much as he had the night of the museum disaster. But as soon as he killed the engine, Annie threw open the door and got out. He was surprised she'd agreed to let him drive her home, but Sonya had helped him engineer the plan. Annie barely spoke to him all the way from his parents'. She pursed her lips and kept her head tilted like she always did when she was mad. He guessed he deserved the cold-shoulder treatment, though he hated it as much today as he had when they were married. Still raw from his father's rejection, he hadn't tried to initiate conversation, either.

He caught up to her at the door. "I'd like to come in."

"I don't think so. I'm tired."

"We need to talk."

"Not now."

That had always been *his* line.

"I'm sorry you're tired. You can take a nap first, then we'll talk."

As he followed her inside, Daisy greeted him with a friendly bark and a warm nuzzle. "I'll take Daisy out."

Rounding on him, she said, "You always resort to bullying."

"When you get stubborn."

She closed her eyes and swore. "I'm going upstairs. Do what you want. You always do anyway."

Damn her, he thought as he leashed the dog.
"Come on, girl. At least somebody's glad I'm here."

He was reading when she came downstairs an hour
later. Her color restored, she looked better. She also
looked mussed, the way she did after they made love.
He felt his body react and covered his lap with the
magazine. "Feel better?"

"Yes. I'm sorry I yelled at you."

"I'm sorry I was late."

"Are you?"

*Don't ask me to apologize for working hard, An-
nie.*

And don't ask me to like it.

"Yes, I am."

Pausing briefly, she finally sat down on the couch
next to him. Her sigh told him the old argument wore
on her, too.

"How did your meeting with Gage go?"

"As well as can be expected. He said he'd let it
be known I was still in the running, and agreed to
wait a while to make a decision."

Pleasure flickered in her still-slumberous eyes.
"Oh, Zach. I'm so glad."

"His keeping me in the running will make a big
difference in my standing in the community."

She reached over and squeezed his hand. "Good.
This is hard, isn't it? The waiting."

"Yes. But I should have been more conscientious about the time today. I let you down again."

She smiled sadly. "In the long run, it doesn't matter."

"It matters to me."

"Why?"

"Because I meant what I told the girls. I want to marry you, Annie."

"There's too much between us, to get married."

"Like?"

"Oh, Zach, the same problems keep cropping up as before. We're so different."

"I think we're making some pretty good compromises."

"Not enough to get married again."

"All right. But at least admit we have a chance now."

"I don't know," Annie said. "Some things can't be fixed."

"You mean Gina."

She winced when he said the name. "Partially. Past hurts have a way of interfering with the present."

"Tell me about it." He saw again his father's granite face.

She stared at him, waiting.

Zach's impulse was to withdraw when the pain hit…

I hate it when you close down on me like that, Zach.

Annie, I'm not like you. It's hard to talk about things.

You've got to find a way. I need for you to share more with me...

He glanced around the room, noticing the stack of baby books on the shelf in the corner. "I want to talk to the baby."

She blinked. "What?"

"Come on. Lean back and close your eyes."

For a minute, he thought she'd object. But she sank back against the couch cushions. He reached down, grabbed her ankles and propped them up on the coffee table. Then he placed his hand on her still-flat belly.

"Hi there, sweetheart," he said. "It's Daddy again." He cleared his throat. "Time for a serious talk."

Annie's muscles tensed but she said nothing.

"This 'being a daddy' stuff's not easy. When you get out here, it will be hard then, too." He searched for the words to explain to his unborn child—and her mother—what he meant. "I don't get along well with my dad, your grandpa. But I did at first. After they had me, my mother didn't have any other kids for several years. My father was great then. He'd come home from work, play with me, take me places. Then my mother got pregnant with the twins. My father started working two jobs, and when he was home, he'd take care of your grandmother most of the time.

She had to stay in bed a lot to make sure the babies made it.''

Zach took in a deep breath, not sure he could continue. He'd never told this to anyone. "When I was five, it was time to register me for school. I sat outside our house on the broken stone steps, waiting for Pa to come home. I'd dressed myself in the cleanest pants and shirt I could find, although I was embarrassed that they were wrinkled. It was August, so it was hot out, and I got sweaty. But I waited there on the steps, sure he would come. It hurt to watch all the kids on the street walk by, holding hands with their moms, laughing as they made their way to the school. It got later and later, but I really believed he'd come. Finally, he showed up, dusty from his job as a foreman at the factory." Zach could still see his father's young face lined with fatigue. "I asked him if he was ready. He said, 'For what?' Still, I persevered. He tried to cover for the fact that he'd forgotten about me, said he needed to check on my mother, then we'd go, and he went inside. I waited another half hour, and finally he came out. We walked down the hill to Saint Patrick's, the Catholic school where everyone on our street went." Zach felt his throat close up. He was five again, facing the stern nun who told his father that registration had filled up. Zach would have to go to Carter School for kindergarten—it was public and couldn't turn anyone away—then enroll next year at the parochial school for first grade. "It was hard not going to school with my friends for a whole year. But it was even harder knowing I wasn't important enough anymore for my dad to have remembered to be in time to get me registered.''

Zach leaned back on the pillows and closed his eyes. He couldn't look at Annie. ''That one incident hurt more than all the others. Probably because after that I steeled myself for further rejection. He missed my eighth-grade graduation because Kent was born that night. He missed the final sectional baseball game because Nora came home from the hospital that day. But the kindergarten thing—that hurt the most.'' Raw emotion flooded Zach. ''I never forgot it.''

Annie covered his hand with hers and squeezed. When he managed to open his eyes, he saw tears in hers. He didn't know until she raised her fingers to his cheeks that his own were wet.

''That story explains a lot,'' she said simply. ''All along, I thought your not wanting your own children was because of the responsibility you had for your brothers and sisters. That wasn't why, was it?''

''No. Not all of it, anyway. The worst part was the neglect. It sounds so stupid now, so trite, but—''

''It's not stupid.'' She rubbed her knuckles on his cheek. ''That's why you were so impressed by your uncle Cary.''

''I know. I was so happy when he moved his architectural firm back to Massachusetts when I was fifteen.''

''And you were his favorite?''

"I was named after him. Apparently he and Aunt Linda couldn't have kids so he took an interest in me. He came to all my games, he took me to his office and I was enthralled by the big drafting tables, slide rules and sketching equipment." Zach smiled. "I remember the first time I went to his golf club. I was so impressed."

"What was Linda's attitude toward all this?"

"She adored Cary. He was her whole life and she'd do anything for him. Anything he asked. She accepted me as a surrogate son as easily as he did."

"She was probably your idea of the perfect wife."

"Could be."

Annie sank back onto the couch. "Everything makes a lot more sense now—where your expectations came from, where you got your ideas for the kind of life you wanted." She was quiet for a while. "I knew, of course, that you were close to Cary before he retired to Florida. But why didn't you ever tell me this story about your dad?"

"I don't know. I'm not sure I ever put it all together until now. But when my father walked out of the kitchen today, it was like standing in front of him on the stone steps and realizing he didn't care enough to remember about school. About me."

"He cared, Zach. He was just busy."

"With the other kids." Zach's hand clenched on her stomach. "I never really did want any children, Annie," he admitted. "I told you I just wanted to wait, but I never really wanted any."

"And now?" Annie asked. "What about now?"

Zach felt as if every nerve ending in his body was exposed. "I want this baby. I swear. I've changed. Your leaving me…the collapse of the building and the death of that woman…I want different things from life now." Studying her face, he raised his hand to her mouth and brushed her lips with the pad of his thumb. "Give me a chance, Annie. Please…"

Annie leaned into his hand, closed her eyes and listened to his hoarsely uttered plea. Could she do what he was asking? Could she agree to try to make their relationship work? It wasn't as though she was agreeing to marry him. Or even sleep with him.

She opened her eyes and watched him as he looked at her. His face was so taut with strain it broke her heart.

He needed her, and Annie knew she needed him. Not only for the baby. Annie needed another chance with Zach. A real one. With promises.

Slowly, she brought his hand to her mouth. She kissed his knuckles. They were scraped and rough on her lips.

"I'm willing to try again," she told him. "We should take it slow, one step at a time, but I want to give our relationship another chance. I want to see if we can make it this time."

"For the baby?" he asked, his voice husky.

Turning his hand, she linked it with one of hers and stared into blue eyes that would always be her undoing. "No, not for the baby. For me. I love you, Zach."

Leaning over, he rested his forehead against hers. She heard him expel a deep breath. He'd been anxious, expecting another rejection. "I love you, too," he whispered.

Annie's throat clogged. Gently, she kissed his eyelids, his jaw, his ear, then rested her face in the crook of his neck. She inhaled, the scent so familiar it made her ache. She kissed him there, too. His hand came up her back. She could feel his mouth in her hair.

He stroked her hair from shoulder to waist, then slipped his hand underneath the collar of her shirt to rub her upper back. It felt so good, so familiar. He eased back on the couch, taking her with him, holding her close against him, keeping the gentle massage. The Chinese masseuse had dealt with Annie's morning sickness through breathing techniques, but had shown Zach pressure points on Annie's neck and lower back to help with the soreness that would be caused by the changes in her body. She closed her eyes again, savoring the strength of his fingers, the tenderness of his hands. Nestling into him, she placed her ear over his heart. It was pumping fast and she smiled. Slowly, she undid two buttons of his shirt and eased her hand inside. Coarse hair, a shade darker than the gold strands on his head, wound familiarly around her fingers. His grip tightened on her waist and he sucked in a breath.

"That feels so good. I love having your hands on me again."

"I always loved touching you." She explored his whole chest, sliding her palm around each muscle. When she whisked his nipples, he stiffened.

"Should I stop?"

"I'll die if you do."

She did stop, for a moment. "I don't want to tease you. I'm sorry Zach, I'm not ready. We need to work some more on our relationship before we get physically intimate again."

"What about the night of the collapse?"

"That was different. We were both overwrought, we both needed comfort. And that night, it felt like life could be snuffed out at any minute."

He waited a long minute. "Don't stop anyway. I'll take a cold shower when I get home."

She giggled, the action shimmying her breasts against him. She moaned and this time he laughed.

"You're gonna need one, too, sweetheart," he said, taking his hand from her hair and moving it to the front of her blouse. "Turnabout's fair play." His hand poised over her shirt. "Can I at least touch you? With some degree of intimacy?"

"Yes. I'd like that."

Still he hesitated. "The books say your breasts get tender during pregnancy. Will it hurt if I touch you there?"

"No...it will feel good."

He drew back and looked into her eyes. His were

dark, dark blue. Releasing the buttons of her blouse, he looked down. For a minute she was aware of the plain, white cotton bra she wore, so different from the wispy, colorful little things he used to love.

"It's a maternity bra," she said into his chest.

"It's beautiful." She rolled her eyes. "You don't like it?"

"Nope."

"Well, then." He slid his hand under the hem of her shirt and flicked the clasp open in the back. "Let's get rid of it."

When he pulled the strap off one shoulder, she said, "You're shameless."

"Hey, you're the one who taught me how to do this in college." Inching his hand up underneath a sleeve, he tugged the strap down her arm, past her elbow and expertly drew it over her hand. "I got great at undressing you underneath your clothes when we were in inconvenient places."

He repeated his action on the other arm.

"Like the front seat of the car in the dorm parking lot," she said as he brought his palm to her chest.

"Your mother's kitchen when she was upstairs."

"Remember the time you stuffed one of my bras in your suit pocket?"

He removed her bra through the opening of her shirt, and said, "The leopard one. I pulled it out in front of my father on graduation day, and he…" The teasing expression fled Zach's face when he looked down at her. "Oh, Annie." His voice was ragged and husky. "You are so lovely."

He covered her breast with his palm. The calluses there abraded the tender flesh and she pressed into it. "Zach…"

He stopped. "Does it hurt?"

"No. It feels good."

He massaged her gently, and just as gently he rolled a nipple between his fingers.

She started. "Oh, Zach." Raising her head, she said, "I missed you so much. I can't believe this is real. That you're here and we're together again."

"I'm here, Annie. I always will be."

"Promise?"

He mouth lowered to hers. "I promise."

CHAPTER SIX

HOW COULD HE MISS the first game of the season?

Annie still couldn't believe it. All through the morning, she'd held on to her faith in him. He'll be here, she thought as the kids donned their spanking-new red jerseys with City Slickers emblazoned in stark white—she wore one too that said Coach—and proudly examined their cleats, bats and gloves. Zach had bought more equipment than they'd ever need. He was generous with his money. Apparently, it was his time that he couldn't spare as easily. He'd already missed the mid-July Community Festival parade, and the game was half over. Still, she was hoping he'd get there for the last innings. Fool.

"Annie, what should we do?" her little team captain asked.

She forced her attention back to the game. "What do you mean, Sam?"

"There's a man on first and one on second. Should we go for it or bunt?"

Annie had no idea.

"Geez, I sure wish Zach was here," the boy said ruefully.

So do I. "I'm sure he has a good reason for not

being here, Sam." *His good reason was probably work.* "Tell the batter to go for it."

Annie watched the play. She'd made the wrong choice, and the side retired with no score. They trailed the other team, five to two.

"What good does it do?" she heard José tell Tommy as they gathered up their gloves. "Ain't goin' nowhere without a good coach." He looked apologetically at Annie, then said with typical ten-year-old disgust, "All the fancy shirts in the world don't make us win a game." The boy spat on the ground and took the field. Eight others followed, heads down, gaits snail-paced.

Discouraged, Annie settled onto the bench. Tommy was right. An insidious fear stole over her. Is this the kind of father Zach would be? Generous with his money but not his time?

At the end of the ninth, the City Slickers had lost by one run. Annie tried to console them with ice cream at the local take-out stand, but the atmosphere was morose. By the time she got home, she felt like crying.

She let Daisy out and made her way to the staircase before she noticed the blinking light on her answering machine. She was tempted not to listen to the message, but she'd given Zach half her heart already and couldn't resist hearing his excuses. *Just like before.* As she pressed the play button, a tiny voice inside her nagged, "Aren't you glad you haven't given it all yet—your body and soul—if this is what it's going to be like?''

"Annie, hi. It's me." He sounded annoyed. "I'm sorry, I'm at the office. The guys I hired to do a mathematical mock-up of the museum design finally called and wanted to get started today. The computerized simulation will give us more information on the collapse. I've been meeting with them all morning. It's…" She could picture him checking his watch. His Rolex. "It's ten o'clock now. I guess you've left. I'm going to try to make it for the game, but I'll miss the parade." He swore. "I'm sorry, honey…" He said a quick goodbye.

Annie switched off the machine, but she couldn't stop the tears. She was feeling better physically now that she was beginning her second trimester, the nausea had abated, but her emotions were still roller-coaster rocky.

"Stupid," she told herself as she let Daisy in, then trudged upstairs and ran bathwater. "This is a stupid thing to cry about. His whole future is at stake. How important is one little game?"

The phone rang as she shed her clothes. She didn't answer it. It rang again as she was stepping out of the tub. She let it go a second time as she donned a white eyelet nightgown.

As she climbed into bed, she put her hand over her belly. "It's not his fault, sweetheart. It's just that I'm disappointed. I thought things would be different this time. Or at least that it wouldn't hurt as much.

But it's really not his fault. We're just so mismatched in our expectations, and what's important to us." Annie sniffled and wiped her eyes. "And this time there's more at stake than just another business deal. This time his whole career is at risk." She patted her stomach. "He'll be better with you, though. He won't miss your games or your dance recitals. I promise."

Spurred by her promise to the baby, when the phone rang a third time, she answered it.

"Hi, honey, it's me."

"Hi." Annie tried to infuse some warmth into her voice.

"I'm so sorry I missed the game. Who won?"

"The Scorpions." She sighed. "I'm not much of a coach, I guess."

"No, sweetheart, it's my fault. I'm still at the office. There was a glitch in the computer program, and the guys just got it under way. We're running the mock-up now."

"I see. So you don't have any information on the collapse?" She was hoping for some good news, at least.

"No, and I won't for hours. I'll be here well into the night."

"Well, good luck."

"I'll call you tomorrow." He waited a moment. "I love you, Annie."

"I know. I'll talk to you tomorrow."

Annie hung up, turned off the light and slid down

into bed. She tried to think of good things—the baby, Zach smiling when she'd told him she was pregnant. He *was* happy about the baby, wasn't he? He would be there for her, wouldn't he? He was going to follow through, wasn't he?

But doubts, like ghosts in the night, haunted her. And, as usual, when she felt the most unsure, when she was the most vulnerable, the worst of her nightmares, the worst of her memories came back. When they'd divorced, and for months afterward, Annie had purposely conjured the memory that would keep her from calling him and telling him she wanted another chance. Tonight she tried to banish unpleasant images, but they came back on their own, taunting her, making her question whether or not she'd made the right choice about letting Zach back into her life…

Annie had cried all day over the vicious fight she and Zach had had. It was another pregnancy scare…and he'd accused her of doing it intentionally this time. They'd screamed at each other until 3:00 a.m. and he'd left for work before she got up that morning. She'd gotten her period at seven o'clock that night and decided to go to his office to tell him the good news. And to make up.

Most of the employees of Belton Associates had left for the day, and there was no secretary in the outer office, which Zach shared with four other junior architects. Light shone from under his door, though it was closed. She reached for the handle, surprised it was locked. Her spine tingled and something made her shiver. Knocking lightly, she said, "Zach, it's me, Annie. Are you in there?"

She thought she heard voices and wondered if he was working with the radio or television on, as he often did. It took an unusually long time to open the door. When he did, she noticed three things about him: his blue eyes were glistening with an emotion she couldn't name; his shoulders were tense; and the buttons on his crisp white shirt were unevenly matched.

Behind him, his colleague, Gina Lawrence, stood looking out the window, her back to them.

"Zach?"

"Annie." His voice was gruff.

Maneuvering around him, Annie walked into the office. A long, supple leather couch took up one whole wall, its upholstery indented. From underneath peeked a pair of forest green pumps. The low coffee table in front of it was oddly angled, its papers pushed onto the floor. Turning to look at Zach's associate, Annie wasn't surprised to see her dressed in a dark green suit.

Swinging around, Annie said, "Zach?" Her voice was thick with tears. "Tell me..." She stopped briefly. "Tell me this isn't what it looks like."

He took a step toward her, his eyebrows furrowed, breathing heavily. "Annie, I...you don't understand. I..."

She scanned his face. It was flushed. Closer now,

she saw long, thin red marks below his jaw, on his throat. Reaching out, she skimmed the scratches. "No, please, Zach…"

"Annie…"

"Oh, for God's sake, Zachary," the other woman said. "At least tell her the truth."

From the brutal words, *one* truth crystallized for Annie. Things could never, ever be the same after this. She brushed past her husband and his girlfriend and fled the office.

Cold from head to foot, Annie sobbed as she reached the elevator. Through blurry eyes, she hit the buttons on the control panel. Zach reached her just as the door opened. Blindly she stepped inside. When he followed her, she shrieked, "Oh, God, no." With adrenaline-induced strength, she pushed at his chest. Since the attack was unexpected, he stumbled backward just far enough so that the doors closed without him inside. Annie never returned home, and didn't talk to him for ten days after that obscene night…

Turning over in bed, she buried her face in the pillow. She willed the images of Gina to go away, but for a long time they stayed with her, until she fell into a fitful sleep.

TWO WEEKS LATER, Zach pressed on the gas pedal, increasing his speed to dangerous limits. When he hit seventy, he forced himself to slow down. No use getting killed. He'd never get to hear the baby's heartbeat that way.

The clock on the dash moved too quickly. Annie's monthly appointment was at ten. He had five minutes to get there. Praying this doctor's office ran behind schedule, as most did, he wound his way carefully through the unusually heavy traffic.

As he drove, he thought about the baby. It was the last week of July and Annie was a full four months pregnant. The baby only weighed about eight ounces and was six inches long, but they figured they'd get to hear the heartbeat today. He'd gone to two other appointments with her, marveling in the sonogram, asking the midwife and the nurses so many questions, they began teasing him as soon as he walked into the office.

Annie would be really ticked off if he missed this.

No, not ticked off. Hurt. The way she'd been about the baseball game.

Something else had been wrong with her though. She'd been withdrawn, moody, and Zach sensed it was more than his missing the game, that it was an old pain, old sadness. He'd tried to take her in his arms, and she'd stiffened. He'd forgotten how that reaction caught him behind the knees. After arguments in the past, Zach had always wanted to make love to be closer, to make things better. Annie, of course, had felt the opposite. She said she couldn't be physically close when she felt so emotionally distant. Later, he read somewhere that this was a typical difference between men and women. But the intellectual basis for it didn't help. He still felt rejected.

Suddenly, traffic came to a halt. Damn! He couldn't even call because he'd insisted she take his car phone, and hadn't gotten another for himself yet.

Thirty minutes later, he swung into the Westside Medical Practice's parking lot. The waiting room was crowded with women of all sizes and shapes, but none of them was Annie.

A nurse at the desk said, "Mr. Sloan. Come on back."

Expediently, she escorted him down a long corridor to an examining room. The nurse knocked and waited until she got the okay to enter. Inside, Annie was seated on a chair, chatting amiably with her midwife, Kathryn. Both women looked up.

Kathryn smiled. "Ah, Zach, glad you could make it."

He didn't take his eyes from Annie. "I'm sorry I'm late."

Annie just stared at him.

"Well, that's okay," the midwife said as she lifted a small black box. "Come on, Annie already heard the heartbeat, but you'll be second. That's not so bad."

Annie's eyes told him it *was* bad.

He crossed the room and knelt in front of his ex-wife. Kathryn placed the handheld device against Annie's stomach.

"What's that?" he asked.

"It's called a Doppler probe. We use it now in-

stead of a stethoscope. It works on ultrasound vibrations.'' Kathryn turned on the instrument.

At first he heard nothing, and looked up at the
midwife, alarmed. She adjusted the probe to the left.

And there it was. *Thump, thump, thump, thump.*
The heartbeat was so fast it startled him. He closed
his eyes to digest the sound of life inside Annie. His
throat closed and he struggled to get hold of his emotions.

After a few seconds, Kathryn turned off the device. ''Pretty wonderful, isn't it?'' she said.

He nodded, not trusting his voice. He glanced back
down at Annie's stomach, the reality of his child
sinking in a little more. ''I don't know what to say.''

Annie closed her hand over his, but still she remained quiet.

After giving her patient last-minute instructions,
Kathryn led them to the reception area. Annie made
her next appointment, and Zach grabbed her hand as
they left the office and walked to her car. They
stopped on the driver's side.

''It's a miracle, isn't it?'' he said.

''Yes.''

The end-of-July sun beat down on them, framing
Annie in a golden halo. Dressed simply in a sleeve-
less black-and-white-checked jumper, she looked
calm and healthy. He knew she was feeling better
these days, but he still worried about her. ''Let's get
out of the sun for a minute.'' He nodded toward the
car. ''I want to talk to you.''

She checked her watch. "I have a meeting in forty-five minutes."

"You're only a little way from your office."

She watched him as if she was trying to make a decision. "All right."

Zach circled her car while she got in and rolled down the windows, then he crowded in the passenger side of her small Toyota. His knees bumped on the dash before he adjusted the seat and turned to her. Automatically, his hand sought her hair.

"I'm sorry I was late."

Staring ahead, she bit her lip. "I am, too, Zach. I wanted you to be there so we could hear the heartbeat for the first time together."

"I wanted to be there, too."

"Can I ask you something?"

"Of course."

"Is this baby really important to you?"

"*What?*"

"Do you really want this baby, or are you just saying that to get me back in your life?"

Anger, quick and potent, flooded him. He withdrew his hand from her hair, suddenly not wanting to touch her. Maybe men and women weren't so different, after all.

"Yes, Annie. I want this baby." His words were satisfyingly clipped.

"Are you sure?"

He glared at her. She was still staring out the windshield.

"Look at me when you're insulting me."

Her expression showed surprise as she faced him.

"Yes, I want this baby. I want you, too. I'm sorry I was late. Spence called a meeting with our insurance company without clearing it with me. I left in the middle of a discussion on the firm's liability, much to everyone's chagrin. But I got caught in traffic, so I didn't get here on time."

"So you missed hearing the baby's heartbeat with me."

"A fact I truly regret."

"Me, too." She glanced at the dashboard clock. "I have to go."

"All right, but *you* tell me one thing. Do you want this to work?"

"What?"

"Between us?"

"Yes, of course I do."

"Then you'll have to stop pushing me away with your innuendos and your physical distancing, your subtle rejections."

Her delicate eyebrows arched. "Are you talking about sex?"

"No, I'm talking about trust. But now that you mention sex, let's put the cards on the table. Sex has a lot to do with trust. To you it's a commitment. It's your way of solidifying a...bond with me. It always has been. I can handle that, though I don't like it and never have." His stomach knotted, he finished, "But

I can't handle the fear that I'm going to lose you if I make one little mistake.''

"Two. You've made two mistakes. Big ones.''

"God, you're stubborn! I explained today's circumstances.''

"Well, you should have left earlier.''

"When do you suggest—dawn?'' Regretting his sarcasm, he tried to gentle his tone. "You're being irrational about this.''

When she remained maddeningly silent, he said, "I'm struggling to hold on to my business, Annie. I told you I'd changed, but I still want to create buildings. If I don't straighten out this museum mess, and court new projects, I'll lose everything.'' He said the rest coldly. "I'd hate to think you were asking me to give up my life's work.''

"I'd never do that.''

"Well, cut me some slack and let me try to salvage my career.''

She didn't say anything.

"And I'll try not to miss anything else important. I blew the first game with the boys, and I'm sorry. But believe it or not, I tried like hell to be here today.''

He was tempted to storm out of the car, but he didn't want her to drive away upset. Instead, he reached over, fastened her seat belt and took her chin in his hand. He kissed her soundly on the mouth, then gently on the nose.

"I love you,'' he said and left the car.

ANNIE TOOK THE STEPS of Lansing Country Club slowly. Though the nausea had completely receded, and she could move fast again, her balance was off. She was amazed at how fast things changed—she was only five months along and not even showing—but Kathryn had told her that cells were dividing quickly around her pelvis. It caused her back to hurt and altered her center of gravity.

Pulling open the heavy glass door, she stepped into a world she'd rejected when she and Zach split up. He loved the ornate divan in the foyer, the crystal chandeliers in the entry and ballroom, the worn but luxurious carpet. He loved the atmosphere, the convenience and the camaraderie of belonging here.

It had horrified her. *Us, in a country club? No, Zach, they're elitist.*

She ducked into the ladies' room—something she did with increasing frequency these days—dismissing the old argument. She had enough new ones to worry about.

Zach had been livid in the car after the doctor's appointment last month. And she probably deserved his anger. In the following days, she'd taken a long hard look at herself and decided maybe she wasn't compromising enough. Maybe she needed to be more understanding about his work, about her subtle rejections, as he'd called them…

After three days of stilted telephone conversations when he'd called to check on her—there were no further spontaneous visits—Annie phoned him and asked him to dinner. She cooked his favorite foods, which he ate without relish. Their dinner talk was perfunctory and uncomfortable. Afterward, she cleaned up while he took Daisy for a walk. When he returned, she suggested they talk to the baby.

He was surprised, but went along with the idea.

"Hi, sweetheart, it's Mommy. You're getting bigger now. The books say you weigh a whole pound. The size of a chipmunk."

"Oh, nice analogy." It seemed his interest in the baby could spark some life.

"Well, she is. Aren't you, Lily?"

"Lily?"

"Yeah. Isn't that pretty?"

"It's beautiful. It was my grandmother's name."

"I know, silly." She looked down at her stomach. "Men can be so stupid sometimes, Lily, but don't worry. They've got their good points."

"Hey, she's too young for that stuff." He smiled, the first genuine one he'd given her all night.

It gave Annie the courage to go on. "Guys are a lot different, Lily. They look at life differently. Sometimes, they get caught up in things that don't concern us, or they exclude us and we feel bad. But, if the man in your life ever does this to you, don't get too upset. Try to understand. And it doesn't mean they don't love us. Sometimes you have to get beyond your own hang-ups about things and see the other person's point of view."

Zach had been moved by her advice to their baby,

and had taken it for what it was—an apology for being stubborn and inflexible, and a promise that she'd try to compromise more...

As she looked at herself in the powder room's full-length mirror, she frowned. Her promise wasn't easy to keep. Three weeks later, this birthday party for Gage had been the next hurdle.

She'd told him she didn't want to go, and he'd reluctantly said he would attend the party at the country club without her.

But letting him down had nagged at her all week. This morning, she'd called to tell him she'd go with him, but he'd been out of the office with clients and she hadn't been able to get in touch with him all day. So she'd made a quick trip to the mall, and had shown up here without his knowledge.

In this dress. The silver-sequined outfit reflected her every curve. It rested flat on her belly—thanks to tummy inserts in her panty hose, but still hugged her bottom a little. Zach would love that. She'd managed to flatten her breasts somewhat with a sports bra so the dress fit okay there, too. Actually, she thought she looked pretty good for five months pregnant, with her hair swinging loose and curly and her eyes sparkling with anticipation at Zach's reaction.

Head held high, she strode into Lansing Country Club's ballroom. Because Gage's birthday party was combined with the Citizen of the Year Award presentation, the room was filled to capacity with almost a hundred and fifty people.

How would she ever find Zach in this crowd of men in black-tie and women in glittering gowns? She'd always hated this kind of fancy event. But being here for Zach made the party tolerable this time, and she was ashamed to recall how often in the past she'd pouted her way through these functions. Zach was right—she could be really stubborn.

Scanning the room, she finally found him. He was at the bar in deep conversation with Les and Marion Corrigan. At least Annie would have one friend here. During her marriage to Zach, Marion and Annie had become confidantes, and Annie had missed her when they'd drifted apart after the divorce.

Focusing on Zach again, Annie tried to view him objectively. But she couldn't—as always, he took her breath away. He'd gotten his hair trimmed, and it was brushed back off his face, accenting his strong features. The raven tux offset his golden good looks as he leaned negligently against the rail of the bar.

"Annie?" she heard at her elbow.

She pivoted to find Martin Mann, drink in hand, staring at her. "Hello, Martin."

He leaned over and kissed her cheek, his hand edging to her waist. She stepped out if its path.

"Looking for Zach?"

"No, I've found him. Nice to see you again." Annie moved away from him quickly. Mann's lascivious eyes and roaming hands unnerved her. And her pulse was already racing as she approached Zach. She heard the deep rumble of his laugh. He responded to whatever had been said, then took a sip of his drink.

"Annie?" Les spotted her first.

Zach whipped around, spilling some liquor on his hand. His mouth dropped. Sensuously, as if he could see through the material, he took in every millimeter of her dress, black stockings and three-inch heels. Then his eyes locked with hers. In them, she saw masculine appreciation and unconcealed hunger. Taking two steps toward her, he reached out his hand. She went to grasp it, but he laced his fingers with hers. "Hello, love," he said, his tone so low, so intimate, so sexy, that it curled inside her like a kiss.

"Hello, Zach. Sorry I'm late."

"I thought you said Annie couldn't make it," Les commented.

"I was wrong," Zach answered, his eyes never leaving Annie.

She leaned into him, her breast grazing his arm. "So was I," she said softly so only he could hear. "About a lot of things."

"I HOPE YOU'RE not planning to try to hold me off tonight," Zach whispered in Annie's ear as they danced under the stars on the patio, the festivities drawing to a close.

She snuggled up to him, telling him for the thousandth time that night, with her body and her eyes, that she wanted to make love with him. Now he needed to hear it from her lips. He kissed them briefly just for good measure.

Batting her lashes, flirting unabashedly with him, she asked, "Why, whatever do you mean, Mr. Sloan?"

He growled into her hair, fisted his hand in the heavy mass and tugged on it playfully. "I mean, Ms. Montgomery, that you can't possibly come strutting in here with that dress on and that Lolita look in those gorgeous eyes of yours and expect me to keep my hands off you." Purposefully, he turned her away from the windows of the ballroom, so he faced the grounds and she couldn't be seen from the club. He inched his hands to her hips and cupped her bottom.

"You haven't been keeping your hands off me."

His dancing halted. "Do you want me to?"

"No. Don't ever stop touching me."

Don't ever stop touching me, Zach, she'd said the first time they'd made love. He remembered looking down at her, poleaxed by the emotions that had swept through *him* at her initial sexual experience.

Is it always like this? With everybody? she'd asked.

No. Not with everybody, he'd told her gruffly. *But you'll never know what it's like with anybody else, so don't worry about it...*

Pulling her tighter, he whispered, "I love you."

"I love you, too. Can we leave?"

Zach noted the sidewalk that went from the patio, around the bar and out to the front. "Do you have anything inside?'' He tilted his head toward the ball-room.

"Nope."

"Smart girl." He drew away and tugged on her hand. "Come on." Leading her carefully down the steps, he found their way out to the parking lot. When they reached his car, he said, "Tell me you didn't drive here."

She sidled up to him, shamelessly pressing herself against his hip. "Why?"

"If I can't touch you on the way home, I'll die."

"I took a cab."

"As I said, smart girl."

He opened the door, stepped back, and as she got in, he patted her fanny. "Did you do this on purpose?"

"What?" she asked from her seat.

"Buy this dress tight enough to make my mouth water?"

"Yes, I did."

Inside the car, he drew her into his arms, though they were awkwardly separated by the stick shift, and kissed her.

When he pulled back, he said gruffly, "Stay on the other side of the car, love."

"Why?" she asked as he started the engine.

Tenderly he reached over and palmed her belly. "Because we have precious cargo here, and I have to drive safely. You distract me too much, woman."

But tenderness fled when they reached her house

and she kissed him passionately and seductively on the porch. They were clawing at each other's clothes by the time they got through the door. As Zach got Annie's dress unzipped, felt her bare skin, he lost all conscious thought. As he yanked the garment from her shoulders, she got his shirt off while her tongue did crazy things to his breastbone. When the dress fell to the floor, he fought with her panty hose.

She pulled away from him. "Zach, stop a minute."

"Not a chance. I want you right here on the living-room floor."

"No, love, I...I have to go to the bathroom." She took a little bite out of his pec. "A side effect of pregnancy."

He chuckled. "All right."

"I'll use the one down here."

He kissed her hard. "Hurry."

But she didn't. When she'd been gone too long, he went to the bathroom door. "Annie?" He heard the toilet flush. "You're not sick again, are you?"

The door opened. Annie was standing before him, in a black sports bra and panties, with a stark white face. His stomach dropped to the floor. "Honey, what is it?"

"It's the baby...I'm spotting."

CHAPTER SEVEN

"SPOTTING IS COMMON during the early stages of pregnancy." Kathryn held Annie's gaze for emphasis.

"I know. You said that on the phone last night."

"You're worried anyway. That's normal. But try to believe what I tell you. The internal exam I just did shows the cervix is closed, which means the baby is fine and not ready to make its debut. I think the bleeding was caused by broken blood vessels."

"From dancing?"

Kathryn smiled. "Maybe, especially since you haven't danced in years. But pressure from the baby or just thinning of the uterine walls could have started the spotting. This usually happens in the third month, but it's been known to occur at twenty or twenty-two weeks, which is about where you are in the pregnancy. You can scoot down now."

Annie slipped to the edge of the examining table.

"The internal shows nothing's wrong," Kathryn repeated. "And as I also told you last night, we've already gotten the heartbeat. That's a very good indicator that everything's all right. Let's listen to it again today."

Holding her breath, Annie waited as Kathryn situated the probe on her stomach. Suddenly, they heard the baby's little heart pump blood through her system. Lily was fine.

Annie tried to quell the tears of relief that stung her eyes. She'd gotten through the horrendous hours of the night—thanks mostly to Zach—and she struggled not to fall apart now. Kathryn said, "Let's cross the hall and do the ultrasound. We'll get Zach for this, okay?"

"Yes."

After talking briefly with them both, Kathryn had asked Zach to wait outside the room while she examined Annie. Though Annie knew he was terrified, he'd been a rock during the whole nightmare.

When she saw him pacing the hallway, she gave him a weak grin. He looked disheveled and distraught, but he smiled at her bravely.

"Kathryn says everything's okay," she told him.

"Thank God." He grasped her hand as the midwife led them into the next room. It took a few minutes for the technician to arrange Annie on the table and set up the monitor. Zach clasped her hand tightly through it all.

The monitoring instrument was cold and covered with translucent gel; Annie flinched when they placed it on her belly. Soon, a black-and-white image flicked on the screen. Her breath caught in her throat as she looked at the picture. It was watery and something moved, almost in slow motion. She could make out two big bumps. It took her a second to realize one bump was the head, one the fanny. The baby was facing down in the classic fetal position.

Annie was mesmerized as Kathryn outlined the various parts of the image. ''This is the halfway point in your pregnancy. The baby is all developed and will just grow from now on.'' She pointed to a movement, fast and pulsing. ''This is the heart. It's beating strong and steady.'' The midwife indicated hands, feet and spine. Another movement and Zach chuckled, his fingers clenching Annie's.

''That's her thumb,'' he said. ''She's sucking her thumb.''

Sure enough, Annie could make out a little curled-up hand, the thumb lodged firmly in the baby's mouth. That small gesture tipped the balance and the tears came. She was really having Zach's baby.

He smoothed back her hair and kissed her cheek. When she looked at him, his eyes were bright. ''It's a miracle, isn't it?'' he said, his voice hoarse.

''Yes. And she's our miracle.''

He nodded.

Kathryn laughed. ''Well, we can't really tell from this angle if it's a she. But there's no evidence to the contrary,'' the midwife said dryly as she pointed to the genital area.

Both Zach and Annie laughed. The levity felt good after the traumatic hours they'd just spent assuring each other that everything would be all right.

"Would you like a picture of this?" the technician asked.

"Of course," Annie said.

"I want one of my own, too," Zach told her.

They finished at the office quickly after that.

"Anything Annie should do?" Zach asked Kathryn before they left. "Or shouldn't do?"

"Well, you two look exhausted. I suggest you take a nap. It's Saturday, so a weekend's rest should work wonders for you both." She hesitated a moment. "And I suggest you refrain from intercourse for about a week. It's probably not necessary, but if the bleeding was caused by broken blood vessels, you should give the walls of the uterus time to heal. Besides, knowing you, Annie, it would scare you to death if you bled more."

Annie and Zach didn't look at each other, both remembering their passion of the night before.

It wasn't until they were in Zach's car, and the adrenaline stopped flowing, that Annie wilted. She sank back onto the seat and closed her eyes.

"You okay?"

"I'm wiped out."

"Everything's all right, honey."

"I know."

They drove home, hands locked together, except when Zach had to shift gears. As they neared her house, Annie tried to block the images from the night before, but they came anyway…seeing the blood, the horrible sinking feeling in her chest when she realized what it could mean...opening the bathroom door, telling Zach and watching reality dawn on him...calling the midwife...Kathryn's assurances based on having already heard the baby's heartbeat...and Zach holding Annie throughout the long and fearful hours they spent worrying if their child would make it.

"No matter what," he'd finally said after examining all the possibilities so many times, they were both overwrought. "No matter what, we'll get through this, Annie." Lying in the semidarkness of early dawn, he'd tilted her chin and said, "If something happens to this baby, we'll have another one. I promise."

Now, on their way home, assured that the child was all right, Annie was able to admit one thing to herself that she hadn't admitted in the last ten hours. Losing the baby would have devastated her. She would have grieved for a long time. But on top of that, she'd feared that she'd lose Zach, too, if they didn't have the baby to hold them together. And that had hurt equally. She squeezed his hand and thanked God she didn't have to deal with either scenario. She promised to try harder at making their relationship work.

The phone was ringing when they entered her house. It was Devon McCade, Zach's associate. Zach took the receiver from her, kissed her nose and said, "Get into bed. Kathryn said you needed to rest today."

Annie climbed the steps but waited at the top.

She heard Zach say, "Yeah, everything's fine…thanks. Um, no, I'm still not going. I don't want to leave her alone yet." A pause. "I know, but it's out of the question. You'll have to handle this alone." After a longer pause, he said, "Damn it, Devon, don't you think I know that?"

Thoughtfully Annie entered her bedroom. She sank onto the bed, where Zach had held her all through the night. Zach, who was fighting for his reputation in the cutthroat business world. Zach, who'd struggled so hard for his success. Zach, who was up against impossible odds until the collapse of the staircase was resolved.

As he stepped through the doorway a few minutes later, she noted the lines bracketing his mouth, the stubble on his jaw. He wore a navy blue sweat suit that he'd had in his car, so different from the tux that lay discarded on the chair in the corner. She remembered ripping at the studs on his shirt to get to him.

He sat down on the edge of the bed. "I feel like I've been through a war."

Smiling in sympathy, she said, "I listened to what you said to Devon."

Gently he ran his knuckles over her cheekbone. "It's not nice to eavesdrop."

"Where aren't you going?"

"Nowhere important."

"Don't lie to me," she said softly. "I want to know."

His sigh was full of fatigue and frustration. "Next week there's an architectural trade show in New York City. Firms set up booths displaying their latest innovations, builders come and do the same. That's all."

"That's not all, Zachary. Spit it out."

"No, it's not important."

"It's important to me."

After a long pause, he admitted, "People looking to hire architects attend."

"So you can drum up a lot of business."

He nodded.

"Have you gone before?"

"Yes."

"How many jobs have you gotten at this trade show?"

"Not too many."

"Exactly *how* many?"

"Four a year." He watched her carefully. "But honey, this time will be different. News of the museum disaster will spread like wildfire through the show. I'm not going to get any jobs until this mess is cleared up."

"It would seem all the more reason to be there."

He looked away.

"That's what Devon said, didn't he?"

"Yeah, but I'm not going."

"Yes, you are. You can talk to people, provide a solid front that Sloan Associates is not to blame for the collapse. If you don't go, you'll look guilty."

"Annie, I'm not leaving you now."

"Why?"

"Because of what happened last night."

"Don't you believe the baby's okay?"

"Of course I do." He messed his hair up even more with restless fingers. "Annie, of all the things we fought about, my traveling was the worst."

"I know." She plucked at the blue-flowered comforter on her bed. "I'm ashamed of how I behaved then."

"It wasn't all your fault," he told her. "I was to blame, too. I was so ambitious. So driven to get ahead, I didn't listen to your needs." He stared out the window. "Sometimes I wonder if that ambition caused the staircase to collapse."

"How?"

"Did I push the innovative design too much? Did I compromise safety for aesthetics to make my mark?"

"Zach, you can't lose faith now."

"It's just so hard waiting."

"When will the report on the beams be in?"

"In the next couple of weeks, I hope."

"Well, in the meantime, you need to do whatever you can to boost your reputation."

He shook his head.

"You're going to New York."

"No, I'm not leaving you."

"Kathryn said to lay off sex for a week."

"What's that got to do with my going to New York?"

"It'll be easier for us both if you're not around."

Giving her a lecherous grin, he raised his hand and caressed her breast. "There are other ways to—"

She shook her head. "No, I want to make love the traditional way. Our first time, when I'm pregnant."

"Annie, that's silly." He cocked his head. "You're just saying that to get me to go to New York."

Her eyes widened innocently. "I'm pregnant, Zach. I'm entitled to whims, to eccentric behavior."

"You're lying."

"Now, don't upset me. Kathryn said I have to rest."

"You don't fool me, Annie."

"You're going to New York."

"No, I'm not." But she could tell he was weakening.

She used her last ace. "Let me tell you what I'll do for a homecoming if you humor me in this." Leaning over, she whispered wonderful, naughty things in his ear.

His face was red when he pulled back. "All right! I'll call Devon."

ZACH REPLAYED the things she said, all the way to New York. He called her briefly Monday morning to tell her he'd arrived, and promised he'd call her at ten that night when he had time to talk. He also told her to be in bed, resting—and naked. There had been a stunned silence on the phone for a second, then she'd laughed, long and low and husky.

It was 10:00 p.m. now. Her phone rang once when she picked it up. "Zach?"

"Hi, baby."

"Hi."

"Are you in bed?"

"Uh-huh."

"Naked? Like I asked?"

"Yes."

"Not even any panties on?"

"No."

"Are the covers pulled up?"

"Just the sheet."

"Is it over your breasts?"

He could hear her suck in a breath. "Yes."

"Uncover them. For me."

She didn't say anything.

Uh-oh. Maybe this wasn't such a good idea. "Annie? Is this making you uncomfortable? Look, honey, I was just—"

"No, Zach, I like it. It makes me feel close to you."

He sighed, relieved.

"I slid the sheet down," she told him.

"Are your breasts any bigger?"

She giggled. "In a day?"

"I wish I could touch them."

"Oh, Zach. I wish you were here."

He moved restlessly on the bed. "I want to be inside you, Annie."

"I want that, too."

He let out an exasperated sigh. "It's late. And this can't go where I want it to. I'd better hang up."

"All right. Zach?"

"What?"

"Call me again tomorrow night. At ten o'clock."

"I'll call you during the day first, so we can chat." He drew in a breath. "Then I'll call you at ten—again."

"Good."

"I love you, Annie. More than anything else in the world."

She was silent, and he cursed what he'd said. The intimacy of their talk had made him forget he didn't want to push her too fast. But the old sentiment, the words they'd used when they first fell in love, the ones they'd had inscribed on their wedding bands, just slipped out.

Finally, her voice husky, she whispered, "I love you more than anything else in the world, too."

"HI BABY."

"Hi." Annie was ready for him the next night at ten. She knew what he was trying to do. Be more intimate. Be closer. Erase all barriers before they made love again.

"Are you in bed?" he asked.

"Yes."

"Are you naked?"

"No."

"Why the hell not? You're ruining my fantasy."

"Oh, I don't think so."

"Annie?"

She loved the note of suspicion in his voice. He'd told her once she was the only woman in his whole life who'd ever kept him off balance. She wanted to do it again. To do it forever.

"Zach, remember how you used to bring me presents whenever you came home from a trip?"

He chuckled. "Do I ever."

"Remember when you went to the Playboy Club in Chicago?"

"Oh, God—the night I came home. I didn't think I'd be able to walk for a week."

"Well, I saved all those nightgowns."

"Annie, please, don't—"

"I've got the Chicago one on."

"It's black."

"Lacy."

She could hear his breathing quicken. "With those little strings for straps," he said.

"I had to sew one." She let the innuendo sink in…let him recall how, in his haste to touch her, he'd ripped the strap.

"Oh, Annie. I want to be there with you."

"Good." She sighed. "Hold that thought."

"Good night, sweetheart."

She rubbed the strap of the nightgown. "Zach?"

"Hmm?"

"I love you more than anything else in the world."

"I love you more than anything else in the world, too."

THE NIGHT BEFORE he came home, he called her for the last time at ten.

"Hi, baby."

"Hi."

"You sound out of breath."

"I just got out of the bathtub."

"Are you wet?"

"Zach, we haven't even talked yet."

He laughed hard.

She smiled into the receiver. "No, I'm all dried off. I was just going to put on some lotion."

"The books said to put it on your belly and breasts to prevent stretch marks."

"All right."

He waited. "Are you doing it?"

"Yes."

"Pretend it's me."

"I am."

"Is it the kind you always used?"

"Roses and Water."

"It's like a flower garden." He remembered vividly the way it smelled, the way it tasted on her skin.

"I wish I was there to give you a massage—all over."

"Mmm. Me, too."

"Lie down on your tummy."

He heard a rustle. "All right, I am."

"Close your eyes."

"They are."

"Imagine my hands on you. On your back. Kneading the muscles of your shoulders, like Felicia said to do."

She sighed.

"Feel good?"

"Yes. You can go lower."

"The small of your back hurts, doesn't it? Because of the baby."

"Yes. I can feel the heel of your hand there."

"Is it good?"

"Very good."

"I could touch you all night."

"Zach, remember what you asked me earlier?"

"Yes."

"I am."

"Good. I'll be home tomorrow night."

"Thank God."

He chuckled. Then, seriously, he said, "I love you more than anything else in the world."

"I love you too, Zach. More than anything else in the world."

ZACH ARRIVED at Boston's Logan Airport at two o'clock on Monday afternoon. He'd caught a plane hours earlier than he expected. Anxious to see Annie, he planned to surprise her at her office, then take her home. They could spend the whole afternoon in bed.

Stopping briefly at a phone booth, he decided to check in with his own office before he headed over to Annie's. Mrs. Farnum, usually calm and cool, was flustered. "Thank God you called in. I couldn't reach you and I knew you'd want to hear this."

Zach gripped the phone. "What's happened? Is it Annie?"

"No. OSHA phoned this morning. The report on the beams came in. They want to see you at three. You'll just make it."

Fear clutched at Zach but he battled it back. "I'm on my way."

"Mr. Sloan?"

"Yes?"

"Good luck."

"Thanks."

All the way out of Boston to Lansing, Zach prayed he wouldn't need luck. Prayed he hadn't made an error in judgment. Prayed the museum disaster hadn't happened because of something he'd done.

By the time he reached Tom Watson's office, he'd made every promise to God he could think of. The secretary ushered him in and Zach once again faced the OSHA executives, the mayor and the city engineers. A technician he'd worked with at the lab was the only newcomer. His heart thundering, Zach took the offered seat and made himself greet everyone politely.

"Well, what did you discover?" Zach asked.

Tom Watson handed Zach a thick stack of computer printouts. "You want to tell him?" he asked the mayor.

"No, you—"

"They held up, Zach," the man from the lab interjected, bypassing the bureaucracy. "We put the beams under the same stressors, for the appropriate length of time. Your specs were accurate. Despite the change order requested by Mann, you were right about the adequacy of the beams."

Through sheer willpower, Zach forced himself not to close his eyes and sigh. Instead, he turned to Watson. "I'm glad the lab bore this out. Just for the record, the independent imaging company I hired to simulate the building's design on computer came up with the same findings. Now, what are you going to do to determine what went wrong?"

"We're starting with the foundation," Watson told him. "Tomorrow morning, we'll figure out how and where to test the depth and breadth of the footings. If they hold up, we'll analyze the soil. That could take a while since we'll need to check a lot of square footage."

"Can I be of any assistance?"

"If you'd meet us at the museum tomorrow, I'd appreciate it. We'll ask Mann and Corrigan to come, too. We need suggestions on whether to go through the building's core or approach the foundation from the outside."

"What time?" Zach asked.

ANNIE CLIMBED out of her car just as Zach's Jag pulled into the driveway behind her. She glanced at her watch. He was early.

He whipped open the car door, slammed it shut and rushed toward her. Without warning, he picked her up and swirled her in a circle, making her denim jumper billow around her calves. Then he gave her a kiss that left her breathless.

"Well, I missed you, too," she said against his lips.

His eyes shone and his face was animated. "I did miss you, honey." He smoothed a hand over her tummy. "And you too, Lily. Hi, it's Daddy." He looked back at Annie. "But there's more."

"Tell me."

"The beams held up."

She sucked in a breath. "When did you hear?"

After he gave her the details, she threw herself back into his arms and he swung her around again. "Oh, Zach, I knew it. I just knew it."

He drew back and stared down at her with a look of gratitude that made her want to weep. "I know you did, Annie. And I can't tell you how much that means to me."

Wrapping her arms around his neck, she said, "Then show me."

A grin of masculine anticipation spread across his face. He bent slightly at the knees and folded his arms beneath her legs. She let him carry her to the door, managed to open it while still in his arms and heard him kick it closed. Heading for the stairs, he asked, "Where's Daisy?"

"The boy next door walks her in the daytime during the warm weather. Sometimes he keeps her at his house to play."

"Great kid," Zach said, kissing her hair, crossing to the steps and taking them two at a time as if her weight was nonexistent. He was on a high from the good news about the building. Annie intended to make him soar.

In her room, the blinds were half drawn, letting in what was left of the early-September sunlight. He slid her down his body, keeping her anchored to him with his hands. "I'm going to love you, Annie, long and slow and so easy we won't hurt the baby." His hand slipped to her stomach and caressed her.

"I want that, too."

Zach held her close. Reining in the wild desire coursing through his blood, he unbuttoned her jumper and let it fall to the floor. He tugged the T-shirt over her head, eased off her bra and slid her panties all the way down her legs. He helped her step out of her shoes. Upright, he ran his knuckles over the upper curve of her breasts, the much-missed feel of her skin making his pulse leapfrog. "Remember those satin sheets your mother gave us as a wedding present?"

She nodded. "You loved to sleep on them."

"Because they were like your skin." His fingertips glided over her. "Only this is softer, smoother."

"I want to feel yours."

He drew back and yanked off his tie and tore at his shirt.

With torturous slowness, she reacquainted herself with every muscle in his upper body. Her fingers fumbled with his belt and pants until he was naked, too. Kissing her way down his body, she breathed the words into his bare stomach. "Six months ago, I didn't take in all these details the way I wanted to."

Fists at his sides, his posture as rigid as a stone sculpture, he let her touch him. When he could bear no more, he drew her up then placed her on the bed. He sat next to her and devoured her first with his eyes. His hands went to her waist. It was thicker, and her abdomen was rounded. He cradled it in his palm. "You're fuller."

"I'm more than five months along. It'll happen fast now."

The image of this lovely belly swollen with his child flowed through him like fine aged brandy, warming him.

He stretched out on the bed, crooked his elbow and propped his head in his hand. He brought a fistful of her hair to his nose. "Mmm, still smells like roses." Locking his eyes with hers, he let the long strands dangle onto her stomach, dance on her delicate rib cage and whirl around a nipple. She shivered.

She turned her head to the right and nuzzled her

face on the inside of his arm. His muscles bulged against her cheek. Kissing them lightly, she pulled his head down and buried her face in the crook of his neck. "Right here...you smell the best. A little sweaty, and musky." She inhaled deeply. "I can just make out the cologne you used this morning. The one that's like the woods in fall."

Zach's whole body bucked. "Annie, I..."

But she didn't let him finish. Instead, she gently shoved him to his back and laid her head on his chest. "I can hear your heartbeat. Strong, steady, sexy."

"How's a heartbeat sexy?"

Reaching down past his waist, she took him in her hand. With the caress, his heart thumped loudly. "Like that," she whispered against his salty skin.

She didn't stop touching him until he grabbed her wrist. "It always amazed me that you were so little I could do this," he said, encircling each wrist with his fingers. His thumb scrubbed her pulse, making it beat faster. Then he glided his hands to the slender slope of her shoulders. "Here, too. So slight. So soft. So feminine."

He moved her up a little for better access and pulled her to him. Annie felt the soft brush of his eyelashes on the upper curve of her breast. Sighing heavily, she relished the whisk of his tongue, the pressure she felt when he closed his mouth over a nipple. Long seconds later, he said, "I love to watch you eat or drink something. Did you know that?"

Her body quivering, she said, "No, why?"

"It's so sexy. I imagine my lips here, like this—" he kissed her throat "—or I think about you taking me inside your mouth—" his thumb grazed her lips "—loving me with these."

In response, she kissed her way down his body and gave him the caress he'd imagined.

When Zach could stand no more, he gently tugged her up and nudged her to her side. Her face was flushed, her eyes a fiery green. Brushing her breasts with his fingertips, he relished her husky murmur, "It's not enough, Zach."

"What do you want, love?"

"Your hands on me. Everywhere. And your mouth."

He did what she asked. He nibbled at the bone on her ankle, kissed the backs of her knees, outlined her ribs with his tongue. He loved her with his mouth until she breathlessly begged for more. He saw her eyes flutter closed.

"No, love, open them."

When she did, he locked his hands with hers, then thrust inside her. She shuddered as he filled her. Zach watched her respond to him, awestruck by the tenderness that came over him. For years, he'd felt like an unfinished jigsaw puzzle waiting for the rest of the pieces to complete him. As her tight, wet warmth surrounded him, as her hands clenched in his, he knew he'd found those pieces, and he vowed never to do anything to make her go away again.

Annie sucked in a breath as he began to move inside her.

On one smooth, slow stroke, her hips lurched forward. "Zach," she pleaded. "More, and not so slow."

"Easy, love, all in good time. Remember, the baby isn't used to this. She's got to make room for me."

Annie's eyes sought his. "There's room for you and Lily both. In my body. In my heart. In my life, Zach."

His self-control snapped. He gripped her fingers convulsively and his body plunged into hers with a gentle force and tender violence that soon erased all teasing, all thought, and all conscious awareness. For them both.

HOURS LATER, Zach roused Annie from a sleepy embrace. "Annie?"

"Hmm?"

"I want to get remarried. Right away."

Her whole body stiffened.

CHAPTER EIGHT

THE NEXT MORNING at the Pierce Museum, the weather turned ugly—just like Zach's personal life. He was still smarting over Annie's reaction to his suggestion that they get married.

Cold drizzle left behind a mist that soaked through his trench coat and seeped inside his shoes. He stood by his car for a quiet moment before the press saw him, and stared at his building. It twisted his gut to see the ravages of the collapse obvious even on the outside of the museum. Before he could catalog all the changes, a reporter spotted him.

Rushing over, the young woman shoved a microphone at him. "Mr. Sloan, what does this mean to you? That the beams held up?"

He gave her a limp smile. "It means no error was made in the design of the foundation."

"Were other errors made in the foundation?"

"That's what we're here to find out."

"Who do you think is at fault?"

"I don't know."

Jonathan Gumby joined them. "What do you think of the Barton family's suit against the museum owners?"

Suit? What suit?

Gumby was quick. "Didn't you read the papers this morning?"

No, I was too busy reeling from another one of Annie's rejections.

Madly piecing together the implication, Zach hedged. "I have nothing to say about Mrs. Barton's family except that they must be suffering greatly over her loss."

Don't say you're sorry, Spence had warned him when they discussed his public statements. *The papers will use it out of context.*

"Excuse me, please," he finished, sidestepping the female reporter.

"Do you consider yourself exonerated, Sloan, now that you know the collapse wasn't caused by the beams?" Jonathan Gumby was becoming Zach's personal albatross.

"I've never considered myself guilty," he said mildly, again heeding Spence's advice. There was always the possibility that they would find he'd made an error in another aspect of the building, but he'd never let his fear of it show.

He had a good poker face, Annie had always told him. Not that it had been in place last night. He shoved from his mind the vision of Annie, sleep-tossed and still warm from their lovemaking, flatly refusing to marry him. It didn't matter that her excuses—they needed more time to heal old wounds, they had the baby's welfare to consider now—made sense somewhere in the part of his mind that was functioning rationally. It still hurt like hell!

Determined to concentrate on this morning's task, he headed toward the museum. At ground level, he saw Mann and Corrigan. As he neared them, their conversation stopped.

"Zach." Mann's voice was neutral.

"Martin." Zach clapped Corrigan on the back. "Hello, Les."

Bloodshot eyes stared at him. "Hi, Zach." Les's gaze darted to the building, then rested on Zach again. "Geez, it was good to see Annie again the other night."

Zach smiled, careful not to look at Mann. If he saw so much as a flicker of lechery in the other man's eyes, he'd deck him. The press would have fun with that one. "She was thrilled to see Marion," Zach told Corrigan.

"They're having lunch this week."

"Oh, good." Just another thing Annie hadn't let him in on.

Tom Watson approached the group. "We're ready to start."

"All right." Zach looked at the building. "What exactly do you want us to do?"

"I'd like to go over the blueprints, to determine where we should dig first."

"What are you starting with?" Mann wanted to know.

"The footings. They seem the easiest to eliminate.

If they follow the spec depths, we'll proceed to the soil.''

''They'll hold up,'' the builder said tightly.

Zach glanced at Corrigan and Mann. Mann had his hands concealed in his suit-coat pockets and was affecting a casual stance. Les's shoulders were hunched inside a blue windbreaker. His lips were pinched.

Who *was* to blame? Zach wondered, as he followed Tom Watson to the prints, donned a hard hat and began examining his design for the thousandth time.

ANNIE STRAIGHTENED Sam's tie and adjusted Tommy's cap. The boys were all dressed up for their Boy Scouts' badge award ceremony. She turned to look at José. The scowl on his face reminded her of Zach. ''I'm sorry your parents couldn't be here for this,'' she told the three boys.

''Don't matter.'' José glanced at the door of the school auditorium. ''Think Zach's coming?''

''I don't know, honey. I told you he had problems with one of his buildings.''

The boy nodded. The two others crowded around to listen. They'd all become attached to Zach. Too attached.

Welcome to the club.

''He's been busy with his building and taking care of his clients,'' she tried to explain. Two jobs that he'd considered in the bag had been lost, despite the decision about the beams.

José scowled again. "Yeah, he don't have time for us, neither."

The sentiment made her uneasy. Annie touched her stomach. Zach had been distant all week. Only yesterday, she'd felt the first real kick inside her, not just the little flutterings, reminiscent of a butterfly flapping its wings. She'd rushed to the phone to call Zach, but she got his machine.

"That ain't fair," Tommy said in response to José's retort. "He didn't miss none of our games after the first one."

"He ain't here, is he?"

Tommy and Sam looked at her.

"I'm sorry, guys," was all she could say.

As her boys left to line up in front, Annie took a seat in the middle of the school's small auditorium. Optimistic, she set her purse on the empty chair next to her. Saving it for Zach. She could still see his utter astonishment, then self-righteous anger, when she'd refused to marry him.

Just because she'd slept with him. How ironic. How typical of them as a couple. Annie had decided to make love with Zach even though things hadn't been settled between them because she thought they both needed the intimacy. And it was something Zach and she had argued about in the past—that she distanced herself physically from him when they disagreed. She'd meant to compromise—but Zach had misconstrued the gesture.

And had lost his temper completely.

The lights dimmed. Everyone stood for the Pledge of Allegiance, then a song, then Annie watched as her little guys got their badges.

At the end of the ceremony, the seat was still empty beside her. José, Sam and Tommy started down the aisle—then raced past her.

And to the back of the room, where a grim-faced Zach leaned against the wall. When the kids reached him, he smiled and squatted. He raised his palm for high fives all around, then carefully examined each badge.

As she walked toward them, she heard him say, "No, I wasn't a Scout. But my brothers were. I remember when Kent earned this climbing badge." He fingered José's colorful patch. "I swear I spent half the summer when I was fifteen going with him on trails so he could get in his miles."

Standing up, Zach came face-to-face with Annie for the first time since last weekend.

"Hi," she said simply.

"Hi."

"Annie, he came." José's black eyes shone with pleasure.

She smiled at the boy then looked back up to Zach's deliberate stare. "I see. I didn't think he'd let you down."

Zach's only response was an arched eyebrow.

"He's gonna take us to McDonald's. Wanna come, Annie?"

"Am I invited?" She put the question to Zach.

"The boys just asked, didn't they?" His response was as chilly as his eyes.

Ignoring the slight, Annie said, "Well, I'm starving so I guess I'll come along."

Across the street at the restaurant, Zach chatted amiably with the kids. The baby kicked once and Annie's hand flew automatically to her stomach. Zach looked at her, his forehead creased. "Something wrong?"

She shook her head, reluctant to share this new development with him in front of the others. He returned his attention to the boys.

Back at the school, he watched the kids pile into her car. "I'll follow while you drop them off," he said, then looked up at the darkening sky. "And to your house. I don't want you to get caught alone in the storm that's brewing."

Lucky break, Annie thought. She wanted to talk to him, and he was volunteering to come to her turf. However, when she pulled into her driveway a half hour later, he didn't get out of his Jag.

"Will you come in a minute?" she asked through the open window at his car door.

"No, I don't think so."

Annie hated ploys, but she hated this distance between her and Zach even more. "I have some things I need moved. I didn't want to lift them."

He frowned—but got out of the car.

Inside, after Daisy made a running leap for him from the kitchen, Annie directed Zach to some boxes that needed to go from the den to the basement. When he was done, he headed for the front door. She grasped the sleeve of his suit coat.

"I felt the baby kick yesterday."

Stopping, he stood still for a moment. When he turned, there was a proud and poignant expression on his face. He reached out and touched her stomach. She held his wrist as he waited. It took a while, but eventually Lily cooperated with a dainty jab right into her father's hand.

Zach's eyes widened and he smiled broadly. He waited until he felt it again, and then drew back. His frown reappeared. "This is playing dirty, Annie."

"I know. I'm sorry."

Still rigid, he said, "Yeah, that's what you said Monday night."

"That doesn't make it hurt any less, does it?"

"No."

"Can we talk about it?"

"We already did."

"No, you lost your temper and yelled. I doubt if you heard anything I said."

His blue eyes deepened almost to navy. "Rejection has a way of doing that to me."

"I didn't reject you, Zach. I simply said I wasn't ready for that kind of commitment."

"You made love with me. I thought that *was* your commitment."

"I know you did. If I misled you, I'm sorry."

"As I said, those words don't mean much right now."

She moved to the couch and sat down. "I'm tired. Please come and sit with me. I'm afraid you're going to bolt if I don't hold on to you."

The corners of his mouth turned up fractionally. "Well, that's a switch. You're the one who's a master at bolting."

He joined her on the sofa.

Grasping his hand in hers, she linked their fingers. He smiled sadly at the gesture and shook his head again. "Why do I let you do this to me?"

"Because you love me. And I love you."

"But you won't marry me."

"Not now." She squeezed his fingers. "I hope we can, someday. I want to be your wife again. It was just too hard when it didn't work out. I need time."

"For what?"

"We have a child to consider now. If we marry, and it doesn't work out, it will affect her negatively. I'd rather avoid the whole thing if we can't make this work. We've got to be sure we've both changed enough."

"I'm trying to show you that."

She thought about the Boy Scouts, and the baseball games, the baby books and the exquisitely tender care he'd taken of her in the first few months. "You are showing me. And I'm trying to meet you half-way. By going to the party at the country club. And by making love. It was my way of compromising.''

Scarlet slashes formed on his cheeks. ''Oh, and I thought it was good for you. I didn't know you did it out of…a sense of duty.''

''Don't be an ass. You know that's not what I meant.''

He studied her for a minute, then sighed, leaned against the cushions and closed his eyes. ''I'm shot. First this, then the business with the building. I haven't slept all week.''

''Take off your coat and shirt, Zach.''

His eyes flew open.

''I'll give you a massage like Felicia showed us.''

''I'm not pregnant.''

''No, but you're exhausted. If I know you, you've been working fourteen hours a day with no breaks.''

''I went to the gym on my dinner hours.''

''Okay, tough guy, lie down and I'll give you a rubdown.''

Zach stripped, settled onto the plush carpet, and Annie straddled him. His shoulder muscles were knotted so she began there. ''It might help to talk about the building.''

''I gave you the gist of it on the phone.''

''What are you feeling about it?'' She ground the heel of her hand into his deltoid muscle.

He groaned. ''That feels great.'' After a minute, he said, ''Something's wrong with Corrigan.''

Annie shifted her hands to his shoulder blades. "Like what?"

"Something to do with the museum, I think. I can't put my finger on it. Did you have lunch with Marion?"

"No, she called and rescheduled for next week. She's opened that boutique she always wanted and she's busy with it."

"How did she sound?"

"Sort of upset, now that you mention it." When he didn't respond, Annie asked, "Have you talked to Les about this?"

Silence.

"Zach?"

"No, I haven't."

"Why? He's your friend. Maybe he needs you."

Again the silence.

"Zach?"

"Annie, I don't want to get in the middle of this. If Les...if Les did do something wrong, it'll come out in the investigation."

"I think you should talk to him. At the very least, you might get more information on the collapse. But mostly, if Les needs you, you should be there for him."

Zach sighed heavily. "Truthfully, Annie, I'm sick of being there for everyone. All my life, I played that role. Maybe right now, I just want to cover my own ass and let everybody take care of themselves."

Annie kneaded his lower back, biting her tongue

to keep from responding. Of course, she believed he was wrong; she thought he should get involved for his friend. But his pique at her refusal to marry him seemed to have diminished, and she didn't want to start a new tussle. So, ignoring the little voice that insisted this was an old argument, that they'd had this disagreement in the past, she leaned over and kissed her way all the way down his spine.

"WE AREN'T GETTING the movie-theater complex," Zach told Devon from his new car phone as he drove back from Boston.

"What happened?"

"Another article in the *Gazette* this morning. Perfect timing."

"I didn't see it."

"I wish I hadn't. It was another of Gumby's rants. It said something about new not always being better and how the cathedrals built hundreds of years ago were still standing...and were safe. He got quite poetic," Zach said dryly.

"What's with Gumby? You ever do anything to him?"

"Not that I know of. He's just doing his job. If a bit too enthusiastically for my taste."

"It sounds inflammatory to me."

"I guess the movie-theater big shots thought so too."

"You coming back to the office?"

"Later. I'm going to stop at my parents' house

since it's on the way. I have something for my sisters.''

Clicking off the phone, Zach felt like throwing it through the windshield. To distract himself, he tried to think of something pleasant—the baby—and for a minute, it worked. It had been more than a week since he'd felt Lily's kick and he was still awestruck. Annie had teased him unmercifully about his reaction.

Annie. Who wouldn't marry him, but made love to him like a courtesan and fussed over him like a mother hen. He wouldn't think about Annie, either.

Turning onto his childhood street, Zach checked his watch. The girls would be in school, but his mother might be home. He hadn't called, figuring he'd just leave the concert tickets in the newspaper box. As he parked at the curb, he took a minute to survey the house. It was old, of course, but it had gotten a fresh coat of paint, and had some vibrant fall flowers bursting out of boxes on the porch. Climbing the stairs to the front door, he noticed for the first time that the steps were no longer slate, but concrete. When had that happened?

He knocked briefly, then eased open the door. "Ma?"

No answer. He trekked into the kitchen. Everything was neat and tidy, if worn. Glancing out the window over the sink, he caught a flash of red plaid. His father, hedge clippers in hand, examined a bush.

Briefly, Zach thought about leaving the tickets on

the table and sneaking out without confronting the old man. But Zach's heart grew heavy at the possibility of his own child someday watching him like this. He'd never want her to leave to avoid him.

His father turned when the screen slammed. John Sloan's normally shuttered face brightened at first, and Zach was struck by the pure pleasure etched there. His father concealed it quickly, making Zach wonder if he'd imagined it.

John nodded. "Zach." Turning back to the bush, he resumed his assessment of it.

Aw, hell, Zach thought, what did he have to lose? "It's lopsided. There on the right."

His father nodded again, raised the clippers and winced.

"What's wrong, Pa?"

"Blisters."

Zach studied his father's back. He was only sixty, but had retired last year. His shoulders were hunched and his arms looked stiff, battle scars from blowing glass in a factory for thirty-five years.

"Want some help?"

The old man started to shake his head—nothing Zach hadn't expected. Then he turned abruptly. "You got your fancy clothes on." His head cocked to the side; Zach recognized the gesture as one of his own. Would his child, John Sloan's grandchild, inherit that trait? "You always get all dressed up like a Protestant?" his father asked.

Zach smiled at the familiar, homey phrase. "Usually."

"Ever hate it?"

Feeling the sun beat down on his head, warming him through the light wool of his suit, Zach said, "Yeah, Pa, as a matter of fact, I do." He glanced at the hedge clippers. "Kent or David got any jeans I can borrow?"

"You really wanna help?"

"Yeah." Zach's throat was tight.

"Go upstairs and change, then."

Ten minutes later, Zach held the cutters in front of a boxwood bush, listening to the sound of his father's voice curl inside him. He hadn't remembered how deep and soothing it could be. Would Lily feel that way about her father's voice?

As they went from shrub to shrub, John was his usual reticent self. But what wasn't usual was the ease of the silence between them. When they were done, Zach checked his watch.

"Don't let me keep you," his father said, the chill back in his tone.

Zach's head came up in time to see the hurt in his father's eyes behind the ice in his voice.

"I'm starving, Pa." On cue, his stomach growled. "I was checking to see if it was lunchtime." He smiled weakly, feeling like a little boy again. After the kindergarten incident, Zach had stopped asking for his father's attention, and rarely let anyone else know his needs. It was easier—when they didn't get met—if no one knew about them. "MacGregor's still have those thick hamburgers with everything on them?"

The utter shock on John Sloan's face shamed Zach. "Yeah," the old man said gruffly. "And those ice-cold beers."

"How about some lunch?" Zach asked tentatively, his heart pounding in his chest. Rejection now would be more than he could bear.

His father waited a long time. "Sounds good," he finally said. "But I pay." He nodded to the bushes. "For the help."

"You're on, Pa."

"HI, LUCY." Annie was seated at a table in La Fondue waiting for Marion Corrigan when her ex-sister-in-law walked in. Annie wasn't surprised. In the past, she and Lucy had met at this restaurant often because it was across the street from the nursing home where Lucy worked. Annie hadn't seen Zach's sister in weeks, though; they'd spoken on the phone but Lucy was still reluctant to accept Zach into their lives again. All the Sloans were pretty stubborn, Annie thought as she looked at the woman who was most like Zach.

"Hello, Annie."

"Are you alone?"

"No, I'm meeting someone."

"How's your job going?"

"Good."

Peering up at Lucy, Annie said, "I wish I could say the same for Zach."

Lucy's eyes flared just like Zach's. "If he's at fault for the museum collapse, he shouldn't be allowed to build anything, ever again."

Stunned, Annie jerked back. "How can you say that about your own brother?"

"How can you be so sure it's not his fault?"

"I know he wouldn't do anything negligent or unethical."

"But he makes mistakes. Take Gina, for example."

Annie's hand sought out her stomach, seeking comfort from Zach's baby. "Are you deliberately trying to hurt me, Lucy?"

"No, I'm trying to get you to see reason." Lucy swept the restaurant with a frustrated gaze. "How are you rationalizing Gina in this reconciliation?"

Gina. Gina. Gina.

"It's not a reconciliation yet. We want to see if we can work things out."

"For the baby?"

If Lucy hadn't mentioned Gina, Annie would have said, *No, because I love him.* Instead, she answered, "Partially."

Marion Corrigan approached the table. "Sorry I'm late, Annie."

After introductions, Lucy gave Annie one last meaningful look and left.

"Are you all right?" Marion asked. "You're pale."

"I'm fine," Annie lied.

When the other woman was seated, and they ordered glasses of sparkling water, Marion smiled warmly. "I can't tell you how glad I am that we're having lunch. How did we ever lose touch?"

Annie lowered her eyes. "It was my fault. I couldn't bear any connection to Zach after our marriage ended."

Marion sipped her water and said bluntly, "Les said Zach told him you were seeing each other again. What happened?"

It was one of the things she always liked about Marion Corrigan. The woman never played games. Never hedged. Annie briefly explained how she and Zach had met on the site of the collapse.

"So, you've been seeing each other since then?" Marion asked.

"Not exactly." Annie blushed. "I'm pregnant, Marion. It happened that same night."

"Oh." The other woman fidgeted with the lapel of her teal jacket.

Annie said, "You don't sound too pleased."

"Are you?"

"Well, yes."

"Annie, are you thinking about going back to him for the baby?"

Puzzled, Annie said, "No, but I'm surprised you sound so negative about it. You always loved Zach."

"I still do. He's been a great friend to Les since college and he also helped him through the AA stuff. Then there was..." She broke off and Annie frowned.

"There was what?"

"Annie, there are some things you don't know."

"What?"

"Are you sure you want to hear this?"

"Yes."

Marion's explanation was delayed when they were interrupted by a waiter who'd come to take their lunch orders.

"Tell me, Marion," Annie said once the man had left, her nerves on edge.

"When you left Zach, he was in bad shape. For a long time. He drank some, and went through severe bouts of depression. Les spent a lot of time with Zach, trying to keep him off the booze, talking to him. We were both worried about him. Finally, Les suggested Zach get some help."

"Psychological help?"

"Yes."

"Did he?"

"No, he refused. What he did instead was retreat more and more into himself and shut the rest of us out. He still had contact with Les, but it was super-ficial."

Moisture welled behind Annie's lids. "I didn't know."

"I'm sure you didn't. He didn't let anyone see the real hurt except us. Eventually, he cut us out, too."

"Are you saying that because Zach cut you out I shouldn't work at my relationship with him? Marion, that's not fair. Zach's always played things close to the vest. I'm surprised he turned to you in the first place."

"He was desperate, Annie. And from your high-spirited defense of him, I'd say your reconciliation isn't just for the baby." Marion smiled at Annie's surprised look. "But that's not what I meant, anyway. I don't want you to go back to him for the baby, because Les and I tried that, and it didn't work."

"What do you mean?"

"You know we have a five-year-old son."

"Yes, Zach told me. You must have gotten pregnant right when I left Zach."

"I did. When they were working on the Pierce Museum, things were really rough for Les and me, too. We'd been talking about divorce. I think that's why we sympathized so much with Zach. Anyway, seeing Zach suffer over your split, we wanted to give our marriage another try. We decided to have a baby."

Annie smiled. "And it worked."

"No, it didn't. When Jason was one, we separated."

"Oh, Marion. I'm sorry."

"We went back and forth for three years. Six

months ago, we sought counseling to try to stop this seesaw.''

"Are you remarried?

Marion laughed. "We never got divorced. The therapist said that in itself should tell us something.''

"So things are good now, between you?''

There were shadows in Marion's eyes when she spoke. "They were going great until the collapse of the staircase.''

"It's caused a lot of stress for everyone. Zach's a wreck.''

Marion didn't say anything, but her eyes welled with tears.

"Marion? What is it?''

"I...I shouldn't talk about it.''

"You can tell me if you want.''

"I'm afraid.''

"Of what?''

"A lot of things.''

"Like?''

"I think that Les is drinking again.''

Something's wrong with Corrigan, Annie.

"Oh, no.''

"That he might be at fault for the collapse.''

Something to do with the museum, I think.

"It's normal to have doubts.''

"And I'm afraid of Martin Mann.''

"Has he done anything to make you afraid?''

"Not directly. Maybe it's just that I've always thought he was a bad influence on Les.''

"Both of us were in agreement on that years ago. Remember?"

"Yes. Unfortunately, we didn't listen to our instincts. And now, I just wonder what havoc he's wreaking in my life."

"Oh, Marion, I'm sorry." Annie reached over and grasped her hand. "Is there anything I can do?"

"Just be my friend. And Les's. Both you and Zach."

CHAPTER NINE

ZACH HIT the punching bag hard. As it rebounded into him, he jabbed it with his other hand. Sweat poured into his eyes, blurring his vision. His shoulder muscles ached and his forearms were beginning to throb. Wiping his forehead with the hem of his half-soaked T-shirt, he took a deep breath and slammed his fist into the bag again.

"Pretending that's Jonathan Gumby?" a voice asked from behind him.

At the last minute, Zach pulled his next punch and pivoted. Martin Mann stood watching him, dressed in trendy workout clothes—navy blue nylon gym shorts and a matching metallic-looking tank top. A terry-cloth band circled his thinning hair.

"Going for a run?" Zach asked.

Though many businessmen belonged to Midtown Health Club, Zach was pretty sure his bumping into Mann at such an odd hour—eight o'clock at night—was no coincidence. Especially since the investigation was reaching a critical point. Officials were expecting the results on the test pits any day.

Mann bent over to stretch his hamstrings. "Yeah,

I've been building up my stamina. I can do five miles. Got to keep up with Muffin.''

"Who's Muffin?" Zach asked without much interest. He turned to the bag and gave it a few light punches.

Mann drawled, ''She's sleek and sexy and twenty-six.'' Zach bet if he looked, the builder's chest would be puffed up.

Tenderness washed over Zach as he thought of Annie's rounded belly. She was a full six months pregnant now and, though the baby weighed only about a pound and a half, Annie needed maternity clothes. They'd had a fight when Zach had wanted to pay for the outfits.

He attacked the bag again hoping Mann would go away. Thoughts of Annie reminded Zach that he was here to work out the problems between them. She still refused to marry him; he was so frustrated by her stubbornness, he'd wanted to punch something. Wisely, he'd come to the gym. He was also trying to sort out their newest conflict—how involved should Zach get in Les Corrigan's life.

Taking the hint, Mann hit the track. Fifteen minutes later, Zach removed his sparring gear and sank onto the bench against the wall. Every single muscle in his body ached and he was still no closer to solving his dilemma. Damn, he wished Annie could let go of things. He wished new issues didn't keep cropping up. He wished that she could accept

him for who he was, instead of wanting him to behave as she would.

She's trying, he told himself.

Yes, she was—by making love when there were
problems between them. She'd glided willingly into
his arms several times over the last few weeks, despite their disagreements. Once, after a particularly
intimate session that robbed him of breath just thinking about it, she'd sleepily admitted that he'd been
right all along—making love brought them closer.

"What's the grin for?" Mann hovered above him.

Glancing at the clock on the gym wall, Zach
asked, "Done already?"

"Yeah."

Zach grunted and stood.

"Buy you a beer?" Mann offered.

"No, thanks. I've got plans."

"I want to talk to you, Zach."

Surprise, surprise. "All right. Let's get some water
out in the lounge before I shower."

When they'd gotten drinks and seated themselves
on a nearby bench, Zach said bluntly, "What is it,
Martin?"

"I'm not sure exactly how to say this."

"Try plain and simple." *And honest.*

Mann wiped his forehead with a towel. "I, um,
know Corrigan's your friend."

"Yes, he is. Is this about him?"

"Uh-huh." Mann took a sip of water. He appeared
truly torn. "I'm afraid he may be drinking again."

"Why do you say that?"

"I've…ah, seen him in the morning a couple of times. He looks hungover."

"You could be jumping to conclusions."

"I hope so." The builder hesitated. "But he's also behaving suspiciously."

"How?"

"He seems anxious—worried."

"We're all worried. I'm anxious most of the time."

Mann caught Zach's gaze and held it steadily. "Corrigan's concern is…I don't know…excessive. Especially about the test pits."

"What about them?"

"He supervised the drilling."

"That's part of his job."

"Yeah, but I was supposed to be there too and I wasn't. Les was on his own for a couple of days when I had to have my wisdom teeth removed."

Zach remembered something about Mann having dental surgery during the digging. He couldn't remember the specifics, as his own life had been out of control at that time.

"Look, Zach, you weren't available a lot when the foundation was laid, with all that was going on with your divorce."

"There's nothing wrong with Les having sole responsibility. He's a good, conscientious worker."

"I hope so. After what's happened, I'm not so sure."

Shaken, Zach eyed the builder carefully. "Did you report any of your concerns to OSHA."

"No, of course not. I wanted to talk to you first."

"Why?"

Mann seemed surprised. "I like Les. And because he's your friend."

"So?"

"I thought I'd bounce my concerns off you. I'd like to avoid false accusations."

"Any more of them could hurt us all."

"I know that. I'm worried about our reputations."

"What do you want me to do with these suspicions?"

"Nothing, really. I just needed someone to talk to about them, I guess." He lowered his head and linked his hands between his knees.

For a minute, Zach wondered if he'd misjudged Martin Mann. This vulnerability was a side of him Zach had never seen.

"Maybe we should talk to Corrigan, see what he has to say," Mann suggested.

Standing abruptly, Zach said, "I'll think about it. I've got to go, Martin. I'm late already."

Trudging to the locker room, Zach shook his head at the irony. If only Annie knew that she and Martin Mann wanted the same thing from him.

"STAY WITH ME TONIGHT," Annie whispered.

Zach eased away from her, bracing himself on his arms, his body still inside hers. He brushed damp hair off her forehead and held her gaze. "Well, some crumbs, at least."

Shadows crossed her face. "Let's not fight, Zach."

"I should be here every night."

"Please."

Sighing, he shifted to his side, bringing her with him. She lay silently in his arms, the tension of her refusal to marry him resurfacing between them like a wall. To scale it, he concentrated on the baby they were going to have in a little more than two short months. Suddenly, he felt a push against his middle. Then a strong, forceful kick.

"What the...Annie, did you feel that?"

She smiled into his chest. "Of course I did."

"It was so strong."

"She's getting bigger."

"But the books said she's still as tiny as my fist."

"Maybe twice that size by now. Her ears are functioning and she can open and close her eyes."

He chuckled into Annie's hair. Each new stage of the baby's development turned him to mush. It also smoothed a lot of rough edges. Aw, hell. So what if Annie wouldn't marry him yet? He pulled the covers around them both. It was the middle of October and the nights were cold.

Their argument banished by a tiny gesture, they lay in contented silence. Annie broke it. "Zach, I need to talk to you."

He kept himself from stiffening. "About what?"

"I've been thinking about my lunch with Marion Corrigan last week."

"You haven't mentioned it."

"I know. I haven't wanted to resurrect all this about Les again."

"Don't resurrect it now, Annie."

"I have to. I like Marion and I want to help her." Then Annie added, "That's what friends are for."

Zach tried hard to ignore the dig, but he wasn't ever quite able to dodge its prickles of pain. "How is she?"

"Did you know she and Les split up a year after their baby was born?"

"At least they were married when they had their kid," he said. He immediately regretted his remark when he felt her body go taut.

When she didn't say anything, he went on, "Yes, I heard about their breakup."

Annie raised onto her elbow. He could see her clearly from the sliver of moon creeping through the partially opened blinds. Heavy-lidded, her eyes held a satisfied expression. Her hair cloaked her like a blanket, tumbling onto his shoulders. "She told me about how they helped you after I left."

Zach sighed and closed his eyes. "I wish she hadn't done that."

Threading her hand through his chest hair, Annie whispered against his skin, "I'm sorry it was so tough for you."

"I thought I'd die."

He felt the light brush of her lips on his breastbone but she said nothing.

"It's why I want us to get married again." He just couldn't seem to leave it alone, kept returning to it like a tongue to a sore tooth.

"Zach, this will either work out between us, or it won't. Being married won't change things."

"I think it will."

"It didn't matter after Gina." She moved to pull away but he held her close to him.

"What else did Marion say?" he asked, trying to change the subject. "How's the boutique doing?"

Waiting a moment, Annie finally settled back against him. "Very well." After another pause, Annie added, "She told me she and Les were having a lot of problems when we split up."

Zach tensed. Corrigan and his wife were having problems during the digging stage of the building. Mann's words came back to him, *Les seems anxious...excessively so...about the test pits.*

"Zach, what is it? You frowned."

"Nothing. I feel bad for Les and Marion. I hope they make it. How are things now?"

"Don't you and Les discuss this?"

"No. I don't talk about my personal life and I don't expect others to."

Annie remembered Marion Corrigan's words. *What he did was retreat more and more into himself and shut the rest of us out.*

"Annie? I asked how they're doing now."

"Things were fine until this business with the collapse."

"Jackson Gage said there were rumors that Les was drinking again."

"Marion's afraid of that, too." Annie hesitated. "She also said she's afraid of Martin Mann."

"Afraid? How?"

"I'm not sure. *Marion* wasn't sure. She's always thought he was a bad influence on Les, but it's more than that now."

When Zach didn't respond, Annie said, "Have you seen Mann lately?"

Another pause. "Yeah, at the gym a couple of nights ago."

"Did he say anything unusual?"

"Look, Annie, I don't want to talk about Mann. It's getting late and it'll lead us to another argument."

Annie could just make out his features in the half light. The familiar line of annoyance on his forehead irked her as it always had. "How can you expect me to let a statement like that go?"

"Because I asked you to." Zach's words were clipped.

"You're obviously keeping something from me. It concerns Les...what we talked about, doesn't it?"

"Damn it, Annie. Give it up."

"No."

He started to push her aside. Tenaciously she grasped his shoulders. "Zach—"

"Annie, let go of me."

She rolled her eyes in disgust. "A few minutes ago, you were furious about my not marrying you. Now you want me to let you go."

"One has nothing to do with the other."

"Of course it does. If you want to work things out, if you want us to get married again, we have to talk about our differences."

His eyes flamed. "No, Annie. We have to accept our differences without trying to change each other."

"Is that what you think I'm doing?"

"Yes." His jaw set, he said, "Like always."

"I just want you to help out your friend."

"You want me to behave as you would."

"As any decent person would."

He shoved her aside, albeit gently. Springing off the bed, he grabbed his pants and stuffed his legs into them. Throwing on his shirt, he said, "You know, this is so familiar. We've had this conversation a thousand times and it always ends up the same."

"And how is that?"

"I always end up feeling like a louse because my value system isn't as good as yours."

As she watched him dress, she thought back to a similar accusation he'd made the first year they were married...

They'd had a fight about an ethical problem at work. Zach suspected one of the junior architects was cutting some corners but felt it wasn't his place to intervene. Annie had told him he had a moral obligation to confront the man. They'd argued vehemently about their values. Later, she found Zach staring into space in their darkened den. When she switched on the light, she saw the sparkle of tears in his eyes. Dumbfounded—she'd never seen him cry—she said, "Zach, what is it?"

He flicked her a glance. "Go to bed, Annie."

Panicky, she'd crossed and knelt at his feet. "What's wrong?"

He shook his head, disgust and pain vying for equal prominence.

"Zach, talk to me."

"No, Annie. No more. I'm not talking anymore to you."

"Why?"

"Because of what you do with everything I say."

"What do you mean?"

"I tell you everything. What I want, my hopes, my dreams. And you know what you do?"

"What?"

"You let me know how shallow they are. How different they are from your lofty ambitions to save the world. When I want a nicer car, or success in my career, you throw in my face what a superficial person I am. When I have values that are different from yours, you make me feel dishonest. Or selfish."

"No, Zach, I don't feel that way about you. We're just different. I love you."

"I know you love me, Annie. You just don't like

me." He looked at her with bleak eyes. "Do you know what that does to me inside? I've let you in here." He thumped on his heart. "I've never let anyone else in here but you. Do you know how it feels when you reject me the way you do?"

Annie had cried, too, for the pain she'd caused him. She'd apologized, rationalized, crawled onto his lap and told him he was wrong about her not liking him. She'd made him believe it, for that night at least. But she'd never forgotten the sheen of tears in his eyes and the deep wrenching hurt she'd caused him...

Annie shivered at the memory. Wrapping the sheet around her, she came to her knees. "Is that what I do to you? Denigrate your values?"

Shoving his feet into his sneakers, he said, "Yes."

"Then I'm sorry. It's not what I mean to do."

"You know, you have to change, too. In order for this to work."

Her chin came up. "I know I do. I *am* changing."

"It doesn't sound like that to me." With one last, meaningful look, he strode through the bedroom door and stomped down the stairs. Daisy barked when he hit the living room. Annie heard soft murmurings, could picture Zach bending down to cuddle the dog.

Swearing, she got out of bed, too. As quickly as she could, she went down the steps and reached Zach just as he grasped the front door handle. Insinuating herself between him and the door, she flattened her palms against his chest. "I'm sorry I've hurt you with my comments. I didn't realize what I was doing. I'll lay off the stuff with the Corrigans.''

He stood still, staring at her. The moonlight peeked in and reflected off his hair. His eyes were as dark as the sky outside. He was trying to resist her, she could tell. After what seemed like forever, his hands went to her waist.

Her naked waist. She hadn't realized she'd come down the steps nude. His fingers flexed on her, then slid down her hips and pulled her to him.

"Please, don't leave," she whispered achingly in his ear. "Stay with me. I love you. You'll make the right decision about Les. I know you will."

His whole body caved in to hers, pinning her against the cold wood of the door. She shivered.

He drew back at once. Bending, he swept her up and started toward the stairs.

She cuddled into him.

Vowed to stop challenging him.

Willed herself to believe in him.

THE NEXT MORNING at seven o'clock, Annie and Zach awoke simultaneously, clasped together like spoons. "What is it?" he muttered into her hair.

"The doorbell."

"Ignore it."

Settling back into him, she snuggled closer.

The ringing continued.

"I've got to get it," she said.

He mumbled something sleepily.

Easing out of bed, Annie donned her robe.

Zach turned over and buried his head in the pillow. They hadn't slept much after his aborted departure, trying with their bodies to bridge the gap their harsh words had caused.

Tired, Annie trudged down the stairs to the living room. Daisy nipped at her heels and barked. "Shh, girl, Zach went back to sleep. Let's not wake him." Quickly, she let Daisy out into the backyard.

At the front door, through the keyhole, she saw her mother pacing restlessly on the porch.

"Mom?" she asked when she faced Sonya—who looked flustered.

"Annie, oh good." Brushing past her, Sonya entered the living room.

"Mother, what is it? Are you all right?"

Sonya headed straight for the television and flicked it on.

"You have to hear this for yourself," she said, switching to a news channel.

A somber-faced man was being interviewed by a local newscaster. Behind him, Annie could see the OSHA insignia on the wall. Immediately, she tensed.

"When was this discovered, Mr. Watson?"

"The subsoil condition was determined two days ago. Late last night, he confessed."

Annie drew in a deep breath.

The screen flashed a picture and a voice-over said, "Late last night, Lester E. Corrigan told OSHA officials that he takes full responsibility for the collapse of the Pierce Museum's staircase seven and a half months ago. Details are sketchy, and none will be released until a full investigation is completed."

"Oh my God," Annie said, covering her mouth with her hand.

"Annie?" Zach's sleep-husky voice came from behind her.

She turned to see him perched on the last step, barefoot, in jeans and no shirt.

"What's going on?"

CHAPTER TEN

ZACH GLANCED at his watch—9:00 a.m. The phone in his lawyer's office rang only once.

"Spence Campbell."

"Spence, it's Zach."

"Did you hear?"

"Yes. It's hard to believe. I'm on my way over to Les's house right now. I got your message when I called for my voice mail."

"Under no circumstances are you to have any contact with Les Corrigan at this point." Spence's usual drawl was urgent.

"Why?"

"He just completely exonerated you in the Pierce staircase collapse. We want to keep it that way."

Annie came into the kitchen, dressed in a loose red-checked jumper with a blouse underneath. Automatically, Zach reached out and ran his hand down her hair.

"Zach, did you hear me?"

"Yes." He stared into Annie's eyes. When she'd left him, Les Corrigan had pulled him out of more than one bar in the early hours of the morning. "Les needs support now." There was silence on the other end. "And Spence?"

"Yes?"

"I *am* innocent. I have nothing to lose by going over there."

"As your lawyer, I still have to object." Spence paused. "But as your friend, I understand what you're saying."

Zach hung up and shrugged into his jacket, feeling Annie's eyes on him. Finally, she asked, "Spence doesn't want you to see Les?"

"No. He thinks it could still hurt me."

She frowned. "Could it?"

"Truthfully?" There was a time when he would have kept this from her to protect her.

"Of course."

"I don't know. But we're going anyway."

Her smile, and the admiration in her eyes, made his heart swell.

On the drive over, Annie was silent for a long time. Then she asked, "How are you feeling?"

"Shocked. Disappointed. How about you?"

"I can't believe it. Les wouldn't hurt anyone for the world."

"Maybe it was just a mistake," Zach suggested as they pulled onto Corrigan's street. "Damn."

Reporters were parked in his driveway, staking out their turf, hovering for the kill. Zach drove down the block and swerved over to the curb. The Corrigans lived on the same street as they had five years ago, so Zach knew the lay of the land well. He and Annie left the car and took the bike path that led around the yards; they ended up at the Corrigans' back door.

After several knocks, Marion answered. "Oh, my God, I didn't expect...what are you..." Les's wife fell into Annie's arms, sobbing.

Annie held on to her and murmured, "It's okay, Marion, we came to help."

Sniffling and mumbling that she couldn't believe it, Marion let them into the house. The kitchen still smelled of potpourri, Zach thought, remembering. Early-morning sun slanted in through the open curtains, bathing the room in golden light. Zach was swamped by memories of how many times he'd come to this house for solace.

Now it was his turn to give comfort.

He said to Marion, "I'm so sorry."

Red-rimmed eyes stared up at him. "I...I don't know what to say."

"Where is he?" Zach asked.

"In the den."

She led them to the other side of the house. The den was dim, and the blinds were half-drawn. Les stood at the window, staring out between the slats. His shoulders hunched like a man of sixty instead of thirty-five.

"Les."

Les turned. His forehead creased when he saw them, then he swallowed hard. "You shouldn't be here."

"Of course we should." Zach crossed to him.

Les's eyes were pained. "You want to know what happened."

"We want to help."

"Sit down." Les motioned to the couch. Zach sat. Marion said, "I'll get coffee."

Glancing from Zach to Les, Annie said, "I'll help."

When the women were gone, Les leaned against the edge of his desk, facing Zach. "Don't you want to deck me? I practically ruined your career."

"My career is intact. I'm here as your friend."

He stared at Zach, disbelief obvious in his tight features. Scrubbing a hand over his face, he said, "Did you know Marion was on the verge of leaving me when we were doing the digging?"

"Annie told me."

"I...went off the wagon after one particularly bad fight."

Zach settled against the cushions. "I didn't know."

"Just once. But it was the night before I supervised the excavation of the test pits."

"And?"

"I was fuzzy the next day. I directed the shovel guys to various spots, but I didn't do a test pit where the beams for the staircase would go in."

"It was on the plans that you did."

"I know. I changed the grid afterward."

"Tell me the rest."

Jamming his hands in his pockets, Les stared over Zach's shoulder. "I didn't realize my mistake until later. Since no subsoil condition was found anywhere else, I figured we were pretty safe."

Mrs. Barton's bloody body flashed into Zach's mind.

"When we dug the foundation, they found a slight problem with the soil then."

"And?"

"It was borderline." His eyes pleaded with Zach. "It was a judgment call. I opted not to report it to Martin or to you."

Zach shook his head. "Les, how could Mann be unaware of all this?"

Les shifted nervously. "I covered it up. I...told the shovel guys it was a minute discrepancy and we had the go-ahead from the builder."

"Why, Les? You made a mistake you could have corrected."

"Because I was drinking, damn it."

"But you weren't drinking on the job."

"No, I wasn't."

"Then I don't understand your reasoning."

"When I did the first test, I was hungover from a binge the night before. Had that become known, I would have been ruined in the industry."

Zach was still unconvinced.

"Besides, Zach, I thought it would be all right. I wouldn't have let it go if I thought there was a real problem."

"That wasn't your decision to make. I'm still confused about why you thought it was."

Les looked surprised by Zach's tenacity. "Maybe my logic was faulty, but it's how I felt then."

"And you're sure Martin Mann knew nothing about this?"

Les eased off the desk and crossed to the windows again. His back to Zach, he said, "Mann knew nothing. Just like you. I put that in writing when I went to OSHA. You're both cleared."

Zach stared at Les. Was it guilt that made his friend's shoulders hunch? Was it strain that caused his fists to clench and unclench?

Or was it something else?

"SOMETHING ELSE is going on here," Marion told Annie as they watched the coffee drip into the glass carafe. She'd given Annie a capsulized version of her husband's story when they'd reached the kitchen.

"What do you mean?" Annie leaned against a bar stool.

"Les is hiding something from me."

"How can you tell?"

Marion faced her. "Can't you tell with Zach?"

"Yeah, I guess."

"He's been nervous and preoccupied for weeks. I know you said everyone was, but it was more than that. I told you last week that there was a problem."

"Yes, you did."

"Since then, there have been phone calls, at odd

hours. Les wouldn't tell me who it was, what the calls were about, but I think it was Martin Mann.''

"Martin Mann?"

Marion nodded.

"Do you think he's involved?" Annie asked.

"I'm not sure."

"Have you asked Les?"

"Of course. I asked him how Mann wouldn't know about the soil problems." She looked at Annie directly. "And Zach, too."

Annie gripped her elbows to refrain from coming to Zach's defense. She knew in her heart there was nothing to defend. "What did Les say?"

"That the architect isn't responsible for overseeing the soil conditions."

"But the builder is." Annie knew that to be true.

"Les said Mann had dental surgery so Les did the supervising alone, but...'' Marion bit her lip and didn't finish her thought.

"But?"

Turning, Marion took cups out of the cupboard. She drew a heavy breath as she pivoted back to Annie. "Look, I believe Zach is innocent. He's a stickler for safety. When Zach was at Belton's, Les always picked on him about overbuilding. If there was even a hint of a subsoil condition, Zach would have insisted topsoil be brought in."

"Yes, he would have."

"And it would have been the builder's expense anyway. Zach would have had nothing to lose."

"He would have done it anyway, Marion."

"I know." She threaded a shaky hand through her hair. "I'm sorry. I've been up all night. I don't mean to say anything bad about Zach." After fixing the tray, she carried it to the table. "But I'm not so sure Mann isn't involved."

"Why would Les take the blame, then?" Annie asked, seating herself at the table. "It doesn't make sense."

Marion sighed. "To me, neither."

ZACH PULLED the Jag into Annie's driveway and shut off the engine. They hadn't said much on the ride home. After talking with the Corrigans for a few hours, they'd left the same way they'd come.

"Want to come in?" Annie asked.

"No, I have a meeting at the office. I'm going to run home first to change." He reached out and rested his hand on her neck. "You know, you've never been to my house."

"I know."

"I don't like that."

"Why?"

"Probably something to do with not accepting me—as I am today." He sighed heavily. "Why does everything have to get so convoluted? Why can't anything be simple?"

"Let's simplify *this*. Invite me for dinner tonight. You cook. At your house."

He smiled, wrapping her hair around his fist.

"You're on, babe." Firmly he pulled her to him for a solid kiss.

Annie drew back, a little breathless. "Do you have a minute to talk?"

"Sure."

"What's going to happen with Les?"

"My guess is he's in legal, as well as professional, trouble."

"How are they doing financially?"

"I don't know. Not well, I think."

"Zach, we should help him out with money."

"All right."

Shifting restlessly, Annie stared out the window. "Let's use that account you set up for me, after the divorce was finalized."

Familiar frustration welled inside him...

I don't want your money. It's blood money, so you'll feel less guilty.

It's your money too. I sold everything we had together and included half of our savings.

I don't want any of it. I don't want anything to do with you or our life together.

"I can barely think about that money," he told her. "I was so angry you wouldn't take it."

"I know. But I couldn't."

"You'll use it now?"

"Yes. Les and Marion are more important than my pride."

"I love you," he said suddenly. "I love the person you are."

Tenderly, Annie kissed him on the cheek. "I love the person you are, too. That's why I'm going to tell you this."

Zach closed his eyes. He was too wiped out to do battle with her again, and he knew one was coming. "Tell me what?"

"Marion thinks Les isn't revealing the whole story."

Zach thought about his friend's edginess, the holes in his story, the kind of man he knew Les Corrigan to be. Damn, why couldn't Zach believe that Les was at fault? Why couldn't this whole nightmare just be over?

Annie eyed Zach warily. She knew him so well, knew what he was thinking sometimes. "You agree, don't you?"

"Why would Les take responsibility for something he didn't do?"

"I don't know," she said. "Are you saying you disagree with Marion?"

"Don't put words in my mouth."

Surprised at his curt tone, Annie drew back.

"Look, Annie, have you thought about the fact that this whole thing could be settled now? I'm completely exonerated and business will pick up again."

"At Les's expense."

"Les confessed."

"You know, I could accept all this better if I didn't feel deep down that you agreed with Marion."

"Truthfully, I don't know what to think."

"So you *do* have some suspicions."

"Annie, you promised me last night you'd lay off." His eyes gleamed with sexual intensity. "In more ways than one, you promised me."

"Everything's changed since last night."

"Yes, I'm cleared."

"You're really not going to pursue this? You're just going to let your friend hang?"

Zach sighed. "I don't know what I'm going to do."

Annie's impulse was to storm out of the car. To tell him she wasn't coming to his house tonight. Then she remembered the hurt in his eyes last night.

The old Annie would have left the car. The old Annie who'd lost Zach. Instead, this Annie reached over and took his hand. She placed it on her belly and closed her eyes.

Finally she said, "Hi, Lily. It's Mommy. Your daddy and I haven't been seeing eye to eye lately. Sometimes that happens, sweetheart, but don't let it bother you. I really want things to work out for all of us so we can live together as a family." She risked a glance at Zach. Holding his gaze, she said, "Daddy's a good man. He'll do the right thing, I know he will. Mommy's got to let him decide what that is...and she's trying." Softer, Annie whispered, "She'll try harder, sweetie. She promises."

A look of gratitude came over Zach's face, so profound that Annie felt tears well. She hadn't realized how much she'd let him down in the past. "I love you, Lily," she said, her throat tight. "And I love your daddy. Don't worry, sweetheart, things will be okay."

ZACH'S OFFICE had been a zoo all day. Since he'd gotten in at two, he'd dodged reporters, refused phone calls and met with his staff, outlining how Les's confession was going to affect Sloan Associates. The atmosphere had been cautiously optimistic. During it all, Zach could still see Les Corrigan nervously pacing his den, having to think twice before he answered Zach's pointed questions. He also replayed Marion's doubts.

Alone now at seven o'clock at night—he'd sent everyone home at six—Zach sat at his desk and stared out the window of his darkened office at the Lansing skyline. Annie would be at his house in an hour. He should leave. Pick up some steaks. She liked croissants—he might still be able to stop at the bakery. A door creaked somewhere down the hall. Swiveling, he looked into his outer offices. Was it Devon? No, he had a date tonight and had said goodbye before he left. Mrs. Farnum and all the others were gone, too, Zach was sure of it.

Chills tickled his neck. He tried to tell himself it could be anyone—a janitor, a deliveryman. Zach started to rise from the desk when a large figure appeared in the doorway. Silhouetted against the half light, Zach couldn't make out the face. Slowly, he reached over to switch on a light.

"No, don't." The voice was familiar.

Zach sat back down. "You into horror-movie ambience, Gumby?"

The newsman came farther into the room. "There's a building across the way. I don't want anyone to see us talk."

"And why is that?"

Gumby looked at a chair. "May I?"

Zach nodded. "This is your show." When the reporter was seated, Zach asked, "Care to fill me in?"

"You celebratin' tonight?"

"Celebrating what?"

"You're cleared."

"I was never accused."

"Like hell you weren't."

"What's your point?"

"You know," Gumby began, taking out a handkerchief and wiping his forehead. "This is so…convenient. Corrigan coming forward. Swearing you and Mann had nothing to do with the museum disaster. A little too convenient, if you ask me."

"Why?"

"Saves your ass. And Mann's." When Zach didn't take the bait, Gumby asked, "Yours need savin'?"

"I just told you it didn't."

"I think Mann's does."

"Why?"

"A hunch."

Zach sat back and folded his arms over his chest.

He said nothing, trying instead to remember something about Jonathan Gumby before this mess with the museum. He couldn't recall anything negative. Hadn't there even been a few accolades?

"I gotta question for you," Gumby said.

"Shoot."

"Know any way this can be checked?"

"Checked? What do you mean?"

"That Corrigan was in this alone? Hard for me to believe the structural engineer took on so much responsibility."

For me too.

"If you know some way, I'll do the legwork."

Zach thought long and hard. He could hear the traffic outside and the clock tick on the wall. Finally, he said, "Mann was having dental surgery at the time the foundation was dug—when the test pits were done."

"Ah. Convenient."

Zach saw Mann's sweaty face at the gymn the other night. "Yeah, I guess it is."

"Easy enough to check. If I had the dates the test pits were done."

Daddy's a good man. He'll do the right thing, I know he will.

Zach could be opening a can of worms. If it got out he helped Gumby, all hell would break loose.

Mommy's got to let him decide what that is...she's got to trust him.

Shoving back his chair, Zach rose and crossed to

the file cabinets on the opposite wall. Opening one, he pulled out a folder. After a quick trek to the copy machine, Zach returned. Crossing to Gumby, he dropped some papers into the reporter's lap.

Without a word, Gumby got up and left the office.

CHAPTER ELEVEN

"BREATHE, Annie."

"I am breathing."

"Not like the nurse said to do it. Come on, honey, watch me." Removing his suit coat and loosening his tie, Zach did the slow-chest breathing technique the instructor had demonstrated and the class participants were now practicing. The hospital's classroom was filled with twelve men and women doing the same drill at the first of six childbirth-education classes.

"Since when did you get to be such an expert?"

Zach bit back a smile. Annie was grumpy and out of sorts lately. Most likely, it had something to do with the fact that she'd gained thirty pounds and had a very pregnant belly these days. He loved it; sometimes, the sight of her big with his baby brought tears to his eyes. "I read one of the books on natural childbirth," he told her.

"You did?"

"Yes, you should, too. I bought three of them."

Annie shifted on the mat, settling more into the pillow, plucking on the knitted maroon smock she wore. "I tried to read one. I didn't get very far."

"Why is that?"

She blew her hair out of her eyes. "I'm scared."

He gave her a sympathetic smile. "You knew that, didn't you?"

Sitting back on the floor, he dangled his hands between his raised knees and looked down at her thoughtfully. "If I were you, I'd be scared, too. This whole thing is new, it's going to hurt, and it's the most significant thing a human being can do—bring another life into the world." His knuckles brushed her cheek. "You have a right to be scared."

The vulnerability in the smile she gave him tugged at his heart. He wished he could protect her from the pain of childbirth. Of course, he couldn't; all he could do was help her through it. "It makes sense to try to confront those fears by admitting them, like you're doing. Denying them would just drain your energy."

"It's been a long time since I've been afraid of anything. Not since we…"

He knew what she was going to say, so he finished it for her. "Not since we split up."

She nodded.

"How's it going here?" the instructor asked as she came around to assist the couples.

Zach smiled at her. "Just fine."

With huge eyes, Annie peered up at the nurse practitioner. "I'm scared," she said simply.

The woman snorted. "Everyone's scared. I've had three kids. I was scared every time. That's what these classes are for. Knowledge is power...the more you know, the less likely you'll be *overtaken* by the fear.''

Annie said, ''That makes sense.''

''Will these breathing exercises really help?'' Zach asked.

Dropping to the floor beside them, the nurse said, ''They can. First they give you psychological control. They take your concentration away from the pain, and help you get yourself through the contraction. They also keep you from hyperventilating.'' She smiled. ''But what will help the most, Annie, is having your husband with you, talking you through the whole process.''

Husband. Zach's insides contracted. He turned away from the instructor and stared out at all the other couples. The *married* couples.

''Well, hang in there.'' The nurse patted Annie's stomach as she got up and left them alone.

''Zach?''

He looked down at his wife—his *ex*-wife. The mother of his child, damn it. ''Yeah?''

''Are you all right?''

''Sure. Logical mistake, wouldn't you say? I *am* the baby's father. I love you to distraction. I'd do anything for you. Why wouldn't she assume we were married?''

Annie laced her fingers with his. ''I hope we will be. Soon.''

Sighing, Zach placed his hand on her rounded

belly. She looked as if she were carrying a football. It didn't seem possible she was only eight weeks away from giving birth. "Come on, sweetheart," he said to the child, "let's help Mommy with this breathing stuff."

Lily kicked him, hard and strong and forcefully. Both he and Annie laughed.

"If you're good and really try to master this technique," he told Annie, "I'll buy you a milk shake at the diner across the street after the class."

"Make that a hot-fudge sundae and you're on."

An hour later, Annie scooped the chocolaty confection into her mouth. She let the warm fudge melt on her tongue, licked the whipped cream off her lips and savored the tart taste of the cherry. When she glanced at Zach, his eyes were riveted on her mouth. "Isn't yours good?" she asked.

"Huh?"

"Isn't yours good?" She hid her chuckle in a napkin.

"Um...my..." He glanced down at his piece of cake, then back up at her. "Are you laughing at me?"

"Yup. But you're great for my ego. I can't tie my own shoes anymore, my ankles are swollen and I waddle. To have you looking at me like you'd rather devour me than that dessert is really flattering."

"Keep the thought for an hour or so," he said, the sexy inflection in his voice causing her pulse to quicken. Then he frowned. "Are you sure it's still okay? The books say some pregnant women have to lay off sex in the last weeks.''

"Kathryn said not until I start to dilate. This week's checkup said all systems go.''

"Well, then, eat so we can get out of here.''

They talked companionably for a few minutes. As always, the conversation came around to the Corrigans. Annie asked, "So, what did Les say when you gave him the money?''

Scowling, Zach cut into his cake absently. "He wouldn't take it.''

"I don't understand. I was sure he'd need it.''

"I was, too. I had a check in my hand, but he refused it.''

"Joel Grayson's his lawyer, isn't he?''

"Yes.''

"Grayson costs a fortune. How can the Corrigans afford him? I just assumed Les used that money to hire an attorney.''

"He didn't.''

Annie shook her head. "This is crazy. I talked to Marion about it. She was clearly worried about money.''

"Les told me he cashed in some savings he had.''

"Marion said they didn't have a lot of savings.''

"Maybe she didn't know.''

"Maybe.''

Annie put down her spoon. "Could someone else have hired a lawyer for him?''

Zach held her gaze. "What are you suggesting?''

"Maybe Mann got him a lawyer."

"That would be nice of him, if he did."

"Or safe."

"What do you mean?"

"If Mann's involved, his lawyer representing Les would cover for him."

"That's unethical."

"So is cutting corners in buildings."

Zach shook his head. "I tried to talk to Mann last week. He was out of town."

"How convenient. When's he coming back?"

"I'm not sure."

A silence stretched between them. Finally, Zach said, "Are you ready to go?"

Annie stifled her comment. "Yeah, I am." Zach's face was drawn in stern, uncompromising lines. Their harsh planes softened her. "I brought a bag in my car tonight. I...thought I'd stay at your place."

His eyebrows shot up. "Why?"

A peace offering. "I noticed when I had dinner there last week that your bed is bigger."

Zach smiled, stood and linked his hand with hers.

"WHAT TIME is your childbirth class?" Marion Corrigan asked Annie as they unpacked a huge shipment of glass figurines in the showroom of her boutique, the Robin's Nest.

"In an hour. I have time to finish up here."

Marion hefted another crate onto a table and dislodged the top. "Is this your second or third class?"

"Second."

"Is Zach going with you?"

"Yeah, I'm meeting him at the hospital."

"How are things with you two?"

Annie unwrapped delicate statues of robins, sparrows and blue jays. "As well as can be expected. He's really angry that I won't marry him, but he's trying not to bully me."

"A tough hurdle for Zach."

"I know." Annie looked down at her stomach, which rested on her thighs when she was sitting. "And he's been great about this whole baby thing. I just can't believe it, since he never wanted kids."

Smiling, Marion set the fragile statues on a shelf. She reached up to switch on a light, then continued, "Les was like that, too. He got so involved with the baby, he was like a different person. It's one of the reasons I stayed with him."

"How *is* Les?"

"Not good." Marion's eyes misted.

"What's happened with the museum?"

"It's slow going. The insurance companies have been meeting. Les's engineering license has been suspended."

Annie reached over and squeezed her friend's hand. "Oh, Marion, I'm sorry."

"The good news is there might not be any criminal charges against him since the subsoil condition was a judgment call." She wiped her eyes and turned back to the crate. Without looking at Annie, she said,

"But I've gone back to Al Anon. Les is drinking again. He's not even trying to hide it."

"Oh, God, Marion, I'm sorry."

"Zach knows."

"He does?"

"He brought Les home one night after they'd been out together. Zach didn't want him to drive."

Zach had said nothing to Annie.

"Last night, Les got drunk at home. Thank God Jason was staying with my mother." She finally glanced at Annie. At her questioning look, Marion said, "Les isn't a pretty drunk."

"He isn't abusive, is he?"

"No, he gets sloppy. Crying. Maudlin." Marion's own tears began to flow and she wiped them with a tissue from her pocket. "Sometimes he doesn't even make sense. I found him at midnight, sitting on Jason's bed, with Jason's favorite stuffed animal in his hand. He kept saying, over and over, something about not having any choice."

"What did he mean?"

Openly crying now, Marion said, "I don't know. He passed out on Jason's bed."

"Oh, Marion, I'm so sorry." Annie rose, crossed to her friend and hugged her. "Is there anything I can do?"

Marion sniffed. "I don't think there's anything anyone can do."

Annie didn't believe that. All the way to the hospital, she told herself there must be something they could do—something Zach could do. Annie tried not to jump to any conclusions about why Zach hadn't told her Les was drinking again.

At the childbirth-education classroom, couples were already practicing their breathing. Each class began with that warm-up activity—Annie hoped she hadn't missed anything else. She caught sight of Zach in the far corner, pacing and checking his watch. His tie was askew and his hands had obviously run through his hair several times. He looked up as she walked toward him. He closed his eyes briefly and his shoulders sagged. Meeting her halfway across the room, he grasped her arm and said, "I was worried. Where the hell were you?"

Ignoring his tone, she said, "I was helping Marion Corrigan at the store." His eyes widened. In guilt? "She was crying, and I couldn't leave."

The instructor asked for everyone's attention, then said, "Let's look at this movie, shall we?"

The film was a detailed and graphic depiction of a real birth. Annie gripped Zach's hand during most of the footage. It was one thing to read about having a baby, and quite another to see it so realistically portrayed. Annie was sweating when it was over. Zach slipped his arm around her, kissed her hair and said, "Don't worry, love. I'll be there with you. We can do anything together."

Moved by her vulnerability, Zach held Annie's hand as they left the hospital and walked to the parking lot. Early November winds had picked up and he didn't think her coat was heavy enough. When they reached her car, he tucked her collar closer around her neck and said, "Come home with me."

She shook her head. "I don't think so. I haven't made arrangements for Daisy."

He watched her closely. Her tilted head gave him the first clue. God, he'd thought they were beyond this. He removed his hands from her and stuck them in his pockets. "All right, let's have it."

She leaned against the car door. "Why didn't you tell me you knew Les was drinking again?"

Zach didn't answer right away. Finally he said, "I didn't want you to get on me about Les, that's all."

"Get on you?"

"Pressure me."

"To do what?"

"To do whatever you think I'm able to in this situation. "

Annie's face flushed. "I'm not *on you* about anything. I just think Les's confession isn't what it appears to be. I want you to talk to him to get to the bottom of this."

"I tried. And he had six scotches."

Annie drew in a breath.

"Annie, did you ever think that pressuring him isn't the best thing to do now?"

"I hadn't thought about that. Marion's really worried about him." Annie shivered.

"What did she say, specifically?"

Annie recounted Marion's description and Les's

vague mumblings. Suddenly, a piece of the puzzle fell into place. Something Jonathan Gumby had said to Zach when he'd talked with the reporter last week. Gumby was still tracking down information on Mann. He'd told Zach he thought Mann might have more to do with the museum collapse than he was letting on. Gumby had also speculated that Les might be taking the fall. But Zach had dismissed the whole idea. What could Les possibly gain by confessing to an act he hadn't committed?

Annie shivered again.

Zach said, "Look, it's too cold for us to have this discussion out here." Leaning over, he opened her car door.

Annie looked at him, her huge hazel eyes concerned. "I've got to go home for Daisy," she repeated.

"So you said."

"You could come home with me."

"I could."

"I want you to."

Zach hesitated. Briefly. Then he met her forehead with his. "So do I."

AT THE THIRD childbirth class, the nurse said, "We're going to talk about the actual birth tonight. Precisely what's going to happen."

Annie looked miserably toward the empty seat next to her. She and Zach had worked hard all week to keep things on an even keel. She'd tried not to push him about Les and he'd said he appreciated it. But there had been a strain between them, a feeling of being out of sync. They'd made love three times, and it had brought them closer, although there'd been a melancholy poignancy about it that frightened Annie.

Sitting alone tonight at the third class, she thought about her life without him in it. God, could she do this baby thing alone? What if he left her now?

"Let's talk about the five phases of labor. They're called early labor, active labor, hard labor, birth and the delivery of the placenta. Coaches, you'll be invaluable here. You'll remind Mom to breathe, give her back rubs, encourage her to push. You might even be the first to see the baby."

Annie glanced around. Just as the tears threatened, she saw Zach in her peripheral view. He spotted her, too, and quickly took his seat.

When she saw his face, her heart lurched. He looked haggard. Lines of worry grooved his forehead and bracketed his mouth. "Are you all right?" Annie asked, taking his hand.

He shook his head. "I'll tell you later." But he held her hand tightly in his and didn't let go.

At the break, Annie practically dragged him out into the hall. "Zach, what's wrong?"

In the harsh, fluorescent lights of the hospital corridor, his face was unnaturally pale.

She clutched his arm. "Zach, you're scaring me. What is it?"

"On the way over here, I got a call on my car phone."

"From whom?"

"The *Lansing Gazette*."

"The newspaper?"

"Well, from one of their reporters. It seems Jonathan Gumby had an accident. He's here, right now, in this hospital. The reporter wanted me to come to emergency."

"What happened to him?"

"A car accident. At least, they say it's an accident."

"Why wouldn't it be?" Annie was puzzled. "And Zach, isn't Gumby the one who's been attacking you in the paper? Why would they call you if he's been hurt?"

ZACH RAISED a glass of scotch to his lips and took a long gulp. He swore into the half-lit, silent office. From the corner, the clock chimed seven times. He was to meet Annie in an hour for their fourth childbirth class.

Propping his feet on the desk, he admitted to himself that his heart wasn't in going to the class. They'd had a beauty of a fight last week. Zach had been so rattled by Gumby's accident, he hadn't censored his words when he'd told Annie the whole story.

Nor had she censored hers...

"Go to the police."

"With what?"

"With the story you just told me about Gumby digging into Mann's actions during the foundation stage of the building."

"I can't go to the police with that."

"Why?"

"Annie, don't you know what this could mean?"

"I guess not."

"Honey, look, if Mann…arranged for something to happen to Gumby, then he's capable of hurting anyone."

"Are you saying you're afraid of Mann?"

He'd reached over and placed a hand on her stomach. "I'm saying I have a lot more to consider now. I won't take any chances with you and our baby getting hurt. I can't go off half-cocked to the police, making accusations that I don't know are true. There's no telling what could result from that."

She'd drawn back and stepped away from him. "Don't you dare use me as an excuse," she told him…

Zach glanced at the clock. He'd go to tonight's childbirth class, of course, but without the absolute joy he usually experienced when thinking about his baby.

Carefully locking his office, he secured the outer offices, too. He fingered the lettering on the outside teak door: Sloan Associates. He remembered how proud he'd felt when the nameplate went up.

He'd believed he had everything he ever wanted.

It will never be enough, Zach, Annie had told him.

At the elevator, he pushed the button for the lobby. The place was still and silent—too early for the night custodians, too late for most of the employees.

The elevator didn't come.

Jabbing the button, he swore and looked at his watch. Seven-fifteen. He still had time. Five minutes later, he decided to take the stairs. God knew he'd worked out enough to be in good shape to go down fifteen flights of stairs.

The stairway was dark. The lights were obviously out. He made a mental note to call maintenance tomorrow. His footsteps clattered on the metal stairs. As he rounded each landing, he was aware of the coolness of the air, the pipes snaking overhead. Unnerved, he quickened his pace.

When he reached the ground floor, Zach snorted at his anxiety. This thing with Mann was really getting to him. Shaking his head at his foolishness, he yanked at the door and it gave way easily. He told the guard about the elevator, strode out the front entrance and crossed the walkway to the parking lot. He was about ten feet from his reserved space when headlights blinded him. Shielding his eyes, Zach couldn't make out who had pulled up in front of him.

As suddenly as they'd appeared, the lights went off.

Zach recognized the BMW right away, and his shoulders tensed.

Martin Mann got out of the driver's side. Ludicrously, Zach noted the expensive leather loafers he wore with his raw-silk suit.

"Hello, Zach."

"Martin. What are you doing here?"

Mann held his gaze. Zach was reminded of a movie he'd seen where the stalker—knowing he had his prey—toyed with him. "I was just driving by and saw you leave the building."

Convenient, Gumby had said. *Real convenient.*

Zach glanced at his watch. "Is there something I can do for you, Martin? I'm meeting Annie in a few minutes."

Mann leaned against the car. "How *is* Annie?"

"She's fine."

"How's her car doing?"

A chill skittered along Zach's spine. Yesterday, Annie's car hadn't started in the parking lot after work. It had been dusk, and her office was in an unsafe part of downtown Lansing. A man walking by had offered to look under the hood for her...

You let a stranger fool with your car?

No need to yell at me, Zach. Yes, I did, and he fixed it in minutes.

Don't ever, ever do that again.

Zach, this guy just happened to be walking by. I didn't go out of my way to get a stranger off the street...

Zach stared at Mann. "How did you know about Annie's car?"

Wide-eyed, Mann said, "Small world, isn't it?

That guy who walked by. He works for me.'' Mann frowned. ''You should tell your ex-wife to be careful, though. No telling who she could bump into that time of night, downtown.''

Zach raised his chin and gripped his briefcase to keep from going for Mann's throat. He knew it was important to remain calm, to think clearly. He stayed silent.

''You've been a good guy to work with, Zach,'' Mann said. ''Things go right now, and when this museum case is settled, I could throw a lot of business your way.''

''I was doing pretty well on my own.''

''Yeah, you were. Wouldn't want that to change, would you?'' Giving Zach a slick smile, Mann opened his car door and turned before he got in. ''Give Annie my best.''

Martin Mann swung into the BMW and Zach watched as the car's taillights disappeared into the night.

CHAPTER TWELVE

"YOUR FATHER would like to make a toast." All eyes focused on Martha Sloan. Though she said the words in her quiet soft-spoken way, the meaning behind them was loud and clear to everyone. Never, in all the years Annie had known John Sloan, had he made any kind of public statement. He hated the spotlight.

Zach's father stood and held up his glass. He looked uneasy, but determined. "I'd like to welcome the newest Sloan into our family. To Annie and Zach's soon-to-arrive baby..." Then he looked at his oldest son. "And to the rest of my family."

Everyone was so still Annie could hear the furnace turn on. Frank coughed nervously and Ben shifted in his seat. Annie opened her mouth to say something to ease the moment, but Zach forestalled it. "Thanks, Pa." He looked around the table, at his brothers and sisters—only Lucy was missing—and said, "To many more Thanksgivings like this."

His meaning was also clear. Zach had come home to stay.

Tears stung Annie's eyes.

"Annie?" Rose asked. "Why are you crying?"

"She's pregnant, that's why," Nora told her sister.

"Do all pregnant women cry?"

"Yes," Martha said. She reached out and squeezed her husband's hand. "Remember when I was pregnant with Zach? I cried over everything."

John smiled. "I worried about that."

"We were so happy about having him."

Annie stole a glance at Zach. She was glad he'd come full circle with his family. But she worried about him. She could explain the tension stiffening his shoulders and etched on his face. The problems between them were wearing on him. But he'd been preoccupied since last night's class. Though he'd seemed to be looking forward to Thanksgiving with his family, he'd been lost in thought most of the morning.

Dinner was loud and boisterous, and Zach got into the mood more as the meal progressed. Annie loved every minute of it. The Sloans had invited both her and her mother to holiday celebrations in the years since she and Zach split, but she and Sonya had never accepted the invitations. This year, she was elated to be a part of their family again, as was Sonya.

"Are you all right, dear?" her mother asked as they cleared the table and brought dishes into the kitchen.

"Yes, just a little tired. I didn't sleep well last night. Why do you ask?"

Sonya hesitated. "You rubbed your lower back several times during dinner."

"I did?" Annie responded.

Sonya nodded.

"I didn't realize."

Annie's mother and Zach's mother exchanged looks, but before Annie could question them, Zach burst into the kitchen. Still lighthearted from his father's toast and the camaraderie with his siblings, he grabbed Annie around the middle—she had no waist now—and cuddled her. "How's my baby doing?"

"Good." Annie put her hand over his. "Kick for Daddy."

Lily didn't. Annie scowled. "She's been quiet all day."

"You look like you've dropped, too," Martha said.

"I have. Kathryn said the baby's getting into position."

Zach patted her tummy. "I can't believe it's only four weeks away."

"Well, I can believe it. Even changing the bed exhausts me."

Martha asked, "Did the midwife say you were going to be on time?"

Annie nodded. "As of Monday, I wasn't dilated or effaced at all. She thinks I'll go to the end of December or later."

"How about some exercise, sweetheart?" Zach asked.

"That's the last thing I want." Annie turned in his arms and rested her hands on his beige cashmere sweater. "How about a nap?"

Zach's eyes darted to his mother. "Later. Let's take a short walk. It's warmed up a lot for the end of November. Just ten minutes." Grabbing her coat and his from the back closet, Zach swept Annie outside before she could protest further.

The winter air was refreshing as they walked along the street where Zach had grown up. Annie could see her breath in front of her, though there was no snow on the ground. Zach held her gloved hand, but was quiet. Annie was silent, too, mildly distracted by a tightening in her stomach. Her hand went to the site of the reaction several times before Zach asked, "Are you all right?"

"Yes. I've been feeling a little odd all day. A little crampy." She smiled. "Braxton Hicks contractions, I think."

"Ah."

"The books say they start about a month before delivery." She patted her stomach through the green wool of the oversize coat Zach had bought for her. "I guess Lily's right on schedule."

"Not scared about reading the books anymore?"

"No. You were right about knowing what was going to happen. It eases my mind." She watched him as they walked a few steps. "Zach, what's wrong?"

"Nothing." His mouth tightened imperceptibly.

"You've been preoccupied since you met me at childbirth class last night."

"The books say fathers start acting strange about a month before delivery."

"Is that all?"

"Yeah, why?"

"I thought maybe something happened with Les."

His pace slowed as he guided her around a patch of ice. "No, nothing."

"Have you given his situation any more thought?"

"Annie, I don't want to talk about this today. I'd like to enjoy Thanksgiving." He smiled down at her and pulled the scarf tighter around her neck. "Besides, I have good news. We got the job for Gage's electronics plant."

"When?"

"The call came yesterday."

"Why didn't you tell me?"

"I forgot."

"Did you get the job because of Les's confession?"

"Gage told me a while back that if I was cleared, the plant job was mine."

"All this makes you not want to rock the boat, doesn't it?"

"Among other reasons." Zach's voice was grave.

"What other reasons?"

"What I told you before about having you and the baby to consider." He stopped walking. The look he gave her was grave and serious. "Annie, I want you to be careful these days." He turned around. "Come on, let's head back."

"How's Gumby?" she asked on the way to the Sloans'.

"He's out of intensive care."

"Have you seen him?"

"Not while he was in that unit. Only relatives are allowed to visit. I'm going to see him tomorrow."

"Zach…"

"Annie, please, lay off. Just for today." Something about his voice caused her to drop the subject. They made the rest of the trip in silence, though they held hands all the way.

Back at the house, Zach led her to the front door instead of the back where they'd come from. When they stepped into the living room, Annie heard, "Surprise!"

Startled, she looked around and laughed. Pink- and blue-covered presents were piled in one corner. Next to the TV towered a five-foot yellow spotted giraffe on which hung tiny T-shirts and sleepers. Big boxes nestled beside smaller ones. Zach's family were all perched on the arms of chairs or settled on the couch or sprawled on the floor.

"Are you surprised, Annie?" Rose wanted to know.

"Very." She turned to Zach. "You're good at keeping secrets."

Ignoring her remark, Zach kept his face neutral.

He'd been struggling all day to act calm and normal when what he really felt was terrified. Had Martin Mann actually threatened Annie? Without revealing his inner turmoil, he hugged Annie and shrugged off his part in his family's surprise.

As they took their seats and Annie began to open presents, Zach's mind drifted back to last night. It was like something out of a bad movie. After considering the whole scenario, he'd decided he'd imagined everything, but the fear had returned. Today, he knew he'd have to make a decision soon. He wasn't letting Annie out of his sight for the entire weekend, but if indeed Mann had threatened her, he'd have to tell her. And together they'd determine what to do about it.

"Oh, Zach, look what your mother made."

Annie held up a stitched quilt with all the *Wizard of Oz* characters on it.

"That used to be Zach's favorite story," Martha said.

Annie blushed. "I know."

Zach squeezed her shoulder. As a newly married couple, they'd watched that movie often, in bed. How many times had they missed the ending?

"I think he just wanted to build Oz," David said.

The front door opened, drawing attention away from the discussion. Zach's jaw dropped when he saw Lucy. She looked around at everyone, then tilted her chin. "I, um, I'm sorry I'm late. There was an emergency at the nursing home, or I would've made it for dinner.''

It was John Sloan who stood and went to his daughter. He hugged her and murmured, ''Lucy. I knew you'd come.''

She hugged him back. ''Yeah, I know you did, Pa. I listened to what you said.''

Annie followed suit, embracing Lucy warmly. But all eyes were on Zach when his sister crossed the room to him.

''Hi, Lucy,'' he said simply from the love seat. ''I'm glad you came.''

She leaned over to where he sat and hugged him. In his ear, she said, ''Me, too.''

After Lucy was settled on the couch next to her father, Rose told Annie, ''Open my present next.''

Annie handed the green-papered present to Zach. He tore off the wrapping and pulled a pink flowered dress and matching booties out of the box.

Martha said, ''I can't believe everyone's so sure it's a girl.''

''You got names picked out?'' Kent asked. Even his distant brother had thawed out because of the baby.

''Just for a girl. We're going to call her Lily.''

Zach's father's head snapped up. He stared at his son, a look so profound on his face, Zach's throat tightened. ''After my mother?''

Zach nodded.

''I don't know what to say.''

"It's a beautiful name," Sonya said as Zach smiled at his father.

Three presents later, Annie opened Lucy's gift. Two books, one for Annie, one for him. Hers was titled *A Child to Love*. Annie read the inscription out loud. "I'm sure you'll make as good a mother as you've been a sister-in-law. Love, Lucy."

After Lucy and Annie exchanged hugs, Zach announced the title of his book—*Being a Father*. He was apprehensive when he read his sister's note on the inside page.

"You've had a lot of experience at this—and thanks to Pa, I've been remembering the good times. You'll be great. Love, Lucy. P.S. Let's talk."

Zach's hands shook slightly as he closed the book. He met Lucy's gaze. Without a word, he rose, crossed to her and hugged her. The emotional moment warmed the Sloan living room.

It took almost an hour to open all the gifts. Afterward, Annie went to lie down. Zach wandered to the basement where his father puttered in his workshop.

As Zach sank onto the bottom step of the cellar staircase, he took in the fluorescent light over the worktable, the coffee mug one of the kids had made and an old yellowed-with-age radio. "You used to come down here a lot when we were kids. I remember you listened to the Yankees games on that thing.''

John didn't look up as he moved a wood saw from the worktable to its home in one of the massive cupboards above. ''It always helped me to think, being down here.''

''I used to think you wanted to get away from us.''

His father's smile was visible from where Zach sat. ''I did.'' He scowled as he placed a screwdriver in a drawer. ''I gave you too much responsibility, Zach. I didn't realize until I talked to Lucy just how much.''

''You talked to Lucy?'' His father nodded. ''That's why she came?''

''Yeah, I guess. At first, she just spouted off. Funny thing, listening to her feelings made me see what we'd done to you. She's been mad at you because you spent so much time with her when she was little, then you went away.'' John sighed. ''I tried to make her see you shouldn't have had to give her that much to begin with.''

''I know you didn't realize what was happening, Pa.''

''No, I didn't. Neither did your mother.'' He tightened the knob on an old wooden drawer in front of him. ''But I see how you could've grown up wanting Cary's life instead. Leastwise, I see that now. Felt left behind, then, though.''

Zach stood, ducking to avoid an exposed pipe overhead. ''Well, *I* see—now—that I jumped the gun a bit on that one." He smiled. "This being-a-father stuff really thrills me, Pa."

His father looked over at him. "It thrilled me, too, son."

The basement door opened at the top of the stairs, cutting off Zach's reply. His mother hurried down. She was smiling but there was concern in her eyes. "Zach, you need to come up. Now. Annie's water just broke. It's time for the baby to come."

ANNIE WAS SETTLED into pillows on one of the twin beds upstairs when Zach reached his old bedroom. She looked tense and scared. It helped to calm him. "Hey, what's this I hear?"

Bravely she gave him a forced grin. "It's time, I guess. Once the water breaks…"

"Yes, I know. Are you having contractions?"

"I've been having them all day. I just hadn't realized this is the real thing."

"You thought they were only Braxton Hicks." He eased down onto the side of the bed and gripped both of her hands.

"Yeah, but they got worse on our walk. I was going to say something, but…"

Tucking a heavy strand of hair behind her ear, he whispered, "Let's not think about that now."

She bit her lip, her hazel eyes wide and fearful. "It's too early, Zach."

"Only four weeks. The baby's fully formed." He

placed his palm on her stomach. "Aren't you, Lily?"
He looked back to Annie. "I'll call Kathryn."

"Okay." As he started to rise, Annie gasped and
grabbed on to him. The muscles in her face went
rigid. "Oh." She drew in a deep breath. "Ohhhh…"

Zach checked his watch.

"It hurts." She closed her eyes and squeezed his
arm tighter.

"Hold on, honey," he said, raising one hand to
the back of her neck, rubbing there.

The contraction lasted about fifteen seconds.

"How many of those have you had?"

"That's the first…really painful one."

"I'll call Kathryn," he repeated.

Twenty minutes later, Annie was sweating as the
third contraction hit her. "Oh, Zach."

"Breathe in, sweetheart. That's it. Now let it out
through your mouth. Nice and easy." His words
were softly spoken though his heart pumped wildly
in his chest.

When it was over, she smiled weakly and lay back
against the pillows. "How long was it?"

"Thirty seconds."

"How long in between?"

"Nine minutes. We go to the hospital when
they're five minutes apart."

"I want some water."

Releasing her hand, Zach stood to go to the bathroom down the hall, when Sonya appeared in the
doorway. Her mother's hair was in disarray and she

clutched the tray she held. "I thought you might want something to drink." Zach took the ice chips and a pitcher, and poured Annie a glass of water.

"How are you holding up, darling?" Sonya asked.

"It hurts like hell when the contractions come, Mom."

"Yes, I know."

"Just sips, honey," Zach reminded Annie as he gave her the glass.

After Annie took a small amount of water and handed the glass to Zach, she asked Sonya, "How's everybody doing downstairs?"

"Good. They're dying to see you, but Martha and I are trying to hold them off."

"Well, maybe you should…Oh, Zach, oh…."

Zach dropped back to the bed and grabbed her hand again. "Let's count now, breathe in… one…two…three…four…" When they finished the slow chest-breathing exercise, the contraction had abated. He reached for the phone.

"What are you doing?"

"Calling Kathryn, honey. That one was only four minutes after the last one. We need to get to the hospital now." He hoped his smile was brave and encouraging and that Annie didn't notice his un-steady hands as he punched in the number. "Looks like we're going to get to see Lily sooner than we thought."

THE PAIN was one big blur when it came, surround-ing her, blocking out all sight and sound. The only other thing Annie was aware of was the tight squeeze of Zach's hand around hers, and his voice.

"That's it, baby, you can do it." Annie breathed in shallow breaths to get her over the top. When the contraction crested, then subsided, her body relaxed.

Zach mopped her forehead. She could feel droplets of sweat run into her hair, which Kathryn had braided. "Good job, love."

"It hurts."

"I know."

"Too much."

"You can do it, Annie. Just get through one at a time—then there are these respites. Remember that. It isn't a string of pain. You've just got to get through the minute."

"That one lasted seventy seconds, Annie," Kathryn said.

"It's getting closer, then, right?"

"Right."

"Move to your side," Zach said. "I'll rub your back."

Annie shifted on the birthing room's double bed, made up with cheerful yellow sheets and a flowered comforter. His hands felt cool on her sweaty skin. "Right there." She looked up at Kathryn who sat calmly in an overstuffed chair. "This is only the second phase?" Annie heard the fear in her own voice.

"We're getting close to hard labor, the third one."

"Your joke isn't so funny now, Kathryn."

"Which joke is that?"

"The one that ends with the punch line…'that's why they call it labor and not picnic.'"

Kathryn chuckled.

Knife-sharp pain lanced through Annie's stomach. It caught her unawares. It was too soon after the last one. "Oh, no, oh…"

Zach gripped her shoulders from behind. She felt his knee sink onto the bed. "Okay, honey, breathe in…a little faster…a little more…that's good, now out…"

The contraction crested, but this time it didn't subside. Instead, it crested again. Annie went rigid and clutched at his arm. "Oh, God, it's coming again. I can't do it, Zach, not again…it's…"

She felt his mouth at her ear, his voice pulling her out of the abyss of pain. "You can do it, Annie. You're the strongest person I know. One contraction at a time…just get through this one. You can do it."

When it was over, her whole body sagged.

Kathryn stood quickly. "That was only a minute from the last one. We're very close now, Annie. I'm going to scrub. I think it could be any time."

She felt Zach ease her to her back and help her stretch out. Every muscle in her body ached. She heard the squeaky crank on the bed and felt herself being lowered. Just as the noise stopped, another contraction hit. The pain devoured her. She closed her eyes and heard herself moan, then yell out. It lasted a long time.

"I didn't want to yell," she said afterward, her voice scratchy.

"I want you to yell," Zach said. "Yell all you like."

Annie looked at Zach. His face was pale, the taut line of his jaw belying his tone. She wanted to tell him she couldn't do this without him. She wanted to ask how he was really doing, if this was hard for him, too. But another wave of pain washed away all concern and she turned into herself to try to ride it out.

Ten minutes later, Kathryn said, "Okay now, Annie, I'm bending your knees. Stay in that half-sitting position." Kathryn's gloved hand pressed on her abdomen. "The baby's moved into the birth canal. I can feel her there." Kathryn paused and looked up. "The monitor shows another contraction is coming."

The room dimmed a little as Annie focused on panting. Then the pain hit. Zach's encouragement drifted through it. "Pant, sweetheart...blow out...pant again..." His voice cracked a bit, and seemed threaded with emotion.

Kathryn said, "All right...bear down, just a little. Good...Annie...good...I see the head...she's crowned...she didn't go back in, so this is going to be it...one or two more pushes ought to do it."

Annie dug her nails into Zach's hand as the next contraction hit on the heels of the last. "Bear down, love, that's it, bear down..."

Suddenly, her lower body stretched. Then it burned. "Oh, Zach...oh, please...oh..."

Zach said, "It'll be all over soon, honey, you can do it, I know it hurts...hold on..."

Kathryn again... "One more push...great, here she comes...okay, I've got her head...don't push again...Zach, tell her not to push, I'm suctioning the mouth...okay...now push again..."

"I can't...I can't..."

"Yes, you can, Annie. I want to see my daughter...you can push..."

Annie pushed.

"There's one shoulder..."

Annie could feel the other...

"Ah, there's the other shoulder..."

Annie felt pressure, sliding... "There...the torso's out...now...oh, Annie...Zach..."

Annie looked down but couldn't see. "What...what is it...?"

Zach said, "It's a girl, love...it's Lily."

Then Annie heard a loud and lusty cry. Bracing herself on her arms, she pulled herself halfway up to behold the most beautiful thing she'd ever laid eyes on. Lily was long and red and wet...and just gorgeous. Annie reached out a hand...she had to touch her. She got a little leg, then Kathryn put the baby in Annie's arms.

She was tiny. Her dark hair was plastered against her head. Her eyes were open and she was looking right at Annie. She was heavy and she squirmed. "Hi, Lily, it's Mommy."

Little Lily watched her with clear gray eyes, then her fist waved, knocking Annie's chin. Annie laughed even as she felt the tears slide down her cheeks. "Still kicking, huh, love?"

From behind Lily, Annie heard, "Here, Dad, cut the cord," but she couldn't take her eyes off her baby.

Lily had red cheeks. They were puffy. Her fingers looked so long. She had dark eyebrows. The end of her nose was turned up.

"Okay, Annie, we've got to get her cleaned up and take care of you." Kathryn reached to take the baby, handing her immediately to Zach.

Before lying down as the midwife told her to, Annie watched Zach take Lily into his hands. He looked at the baby, then pulled her wet, red body to his chest. Tears glazed his cheeks, too, as bent to kiss her. "Hi, Lily, this is Daddy. Remember me?"

AN HOUR LATER, the three of them were alone in the birthing room. For the first time, Zach noticed its coziness—the pictures on the walls, the warm, homey atmosphere, the stuffed furniture. The perfect setting for their family to get acquainted. From the foot of her bed, he watched as Annie put Lily to her breast. The tiny mouth opened and latched on right away. Then she began sucking. Zach chuckled. His heart was bursting with love for them both.

Annie looked up at him. "It's a miracle, isn't it?"

"Yeah." His voice was husky with emotion. Coming around to the side of the bed, he leaned over and kissed Annie on the forehead. She was bedraggled—her damp hair framing her still-sweaty face, lines of exhaustion around her mouth and eyes. But she was never more beautiful to him. Staring down at his child suckling her, his throat tightened. "Thanks for giving me my daughter." He smiled, then said thickly, "You did great, little girl."

Annie reached out to take his hand and kissed it. "So did you, hotshot." Laying her head back against the pillow, she watched him as he sat on the edge of the bed. "I couldn't have done it without you, Zach." She drew in a shaky breath. "I know I couldn't have."

"That's what fathers are for." He scowled. "I almost couldn't bear it, though, Annie. You were in such pain. I...cried."

"I don't remember. Actually, I don't remember much. Did I say anything awful?"

He grinned and, unable to stop touching her, smoothed wisps of hair off her face. "You mean, like damning me to hell for getting you into this predicament?"

"*Did I?*"

"No, sweetheart, you didn't. It was just like the

books said, you behaved in keeping with your normal way of handling stress.''

"What was that?"

"You were mad at being out of control. And you were strong and brave throughout more pain than I could ever have endured." He brushed her cheek with his fingertips. "A couple of times you said you couldn't do it."

Her eyes widened. "And you said I could. That I could do anything. I remember that."

"And I was right."

Annie glanced back down at the baby. She'd fallen asleep, her mouth still latched on to the nipple. Carefully, Annie broke the connection and raised the infant to burp her.

"May I?" Zach asked, overwhelmed by the need to hold his child.

"Of course."

Because he'd had a lot of training in his early life, he easily took the baby into his hands. He felt so…big…holding her, cradling her against his chest. Slowly he rubbed her back. Looking over at Annie, he saw tears sparkle in her eyes. He felt his own moisten again. "I still can't believe it."

"Neither can I."

Zach was disappointed when Lily burped because he had to give her back. Before he did, he held his daughter in front of him for a moment and saw her eyes were open; she stared up at him. "Hi, princess.

It's me—Daddy. I know you can't really see me, but you can hear me, can't you? You know who I am, don't you?''

She was still for a moment, continuing to stare at him. Then she nudged his chest with her foot just as she'd done when she was inside Annie. Regretfully, he gave her to her mother. After Annie settled her onto the other breast, she reached out and took Zach's hand a second time. "Zach?"

Dragging his eyes from Lily, he said, "Hmm?"

"Thank you. For being here with me." Her eyes glazed. "For helping me through this."

He smiled.

"I told you, Annie, I'll always be here for you."

"I know."

At that moment, Zach realized Annie finally believed he meant it.

ANNIE FELL ASLEEP around midnight and the staff took Lily to the nursery for a while. They told Zach to go home. Mother and child needed sleep. And so did Dad, they said.

At the elevator, Zach stopped dead. Next to it, Jonathan Gumby was leaning heavily against the wall. Dressed in a brown flannel bathrobe, his face was covered with bluish bruises, his eyes were sunken and he looked shaky. Zach hurried to him. "My God, man, what are you doing out of bed?"

Gumby gave him a weak smile. "I heard about your baby, Sloan. Congratulations." He swayed on his feet.

Zach told him, "Look, let me help you back to your room."

"Okay. I wanna talk to you. Private will be better."

Worried, Zach assisted the reporter into the elevator and escorted him back to his room. Once there, Gumby shut the door. He dropped onto the bed and laid his head wearily against the pillows.

"You all right?" Zach asked. "Should I get the doctor?"

"No, don't. I'm all right. Give me a minute."

Zach sank onto a straight chair, exhaustion catching up to him.

"I had a car accident."

"So I heard." After a pause, Zach said meaningfully, "What happened?"

"I was reaching behind the seat for a pack of cigarettes. I lost control of the car."

"You sure that was the reason?"

"Yeah, I'm sure. I did wonder whether maybe somebody had messed with the steering column, but nobody had any reason to." He paused, then, "I finally got the report from Mann's dentist."

Zach's body tightened. "Yeah?"

"I got the surgeon's log." Gumby glanced around. "From right here in this hospital. It said Mann was scheduled for surgery at ten o'clock on the twelfth of October. Your records indicate the test pits were done that day."

"So he really wasn't there the day the pits were dug?"

"Nope, not according to the logs." Gumby scowled. "I was so sure about this one. I'm gonna check out one more thing. The doctor was out of town right up until that day. I wanna check the flights and stuff—that's where I was going when this happened." He shook his head. "But doesn't seem likely that anything's gonna come up."

Staring at Gumby, Zach tried to internalize the new information. Had this whole thing been a mistake? Had he misjudged Mann's innuendo? Should he tell Gumby about what he'd feared?

"What's going on here?" Zach was startled out of his reflection by the nurse's voice coming from the doorway.

"Nothin', honey," Gumby said sleepily. "My buddy here, his wife just had a baby and stopped to tell me the good news."

The nurse clucked. "Not tonight, Mr. Gumby. You're still a sick man."

"Sorry," Zach said, standing up. "I'll be going now."

"Take it easy, Sloan."

"You, too."

"I'll be in touch, once I'm out of here."

Outside Gumby's door, Zach sagged against the wall. Could it be true? Had this all been a product of Jonathan Gumby's imagination?

No, you had your own doubts, even before Gumby.

Then there were Marion's concerns.

And what about that thing with Annie's car?

Zach made his way to the elevator, but instead of going to the lobby, he pressed the button for the maternity floor. The night sounds of the hospital echoed around him—hushed voices, a toilet flushing, the ringing of a phone.

Unnoticed, he made his way to the nursery. Through the glass, he found the bed labeled Montgomery-Sloan.

Lily was asleep. She lay nestled in her cubicle, her fanny poking up in the air. Her face was pressed into the mattress. Her hands had come out of the swaddled blankets and were fisted. Zach was overcome by a feeling of protectiveness so great it rocked him.

His mind clicked with the facts: he was taking the week off to stay with Annie and the baby. He'd be with them the entire time. But what about when he went back to work? Would they really be all right? Gumby seemed to think he'd been wrong. Les had confessed.

But staring at the tiny bundle in front of him, Zach decided he needed more proof.

And he thought he knew just how to get it.

CHAPTER THIRTEEN

THREE TEN-YEAR-OLD boys faced Annie by the couch where she sat holding Lily. They shifted from one foot to the other, and tugged on their shirt collars. Annie smiled at their nervousness.

"You gonna always dress her in pink?" Tommy asked.

"She's a girl, dummy," José put in. "They always put girls in pink."

"She has a lot of different clothes," Annie said. "Well, what do you think of her?"

"Kinda red."

"And little."

"I think she's beautiful," Zach said from behind them. "Okay guys, here's some cookies and milk. Dig in."

"You her daddy," José told Zach. "You gotta think she's beautiful."

Sam, who'd said very little, munched his cookies, then nailed Zach with a very adult look. "What's her last name?"

A muscle pulsed in Zach's throat. "Montgomery-Sloan."

"You and Annie? You still ain't married?" the little boy asked.

José kicked Sam.

"I was just askin'," Sam said.

"It's all right, José." Annie turned to Sam. "No, we're not married yet, Sam."

"How come?"

"For a lot of complicated reasons."

Sam looked at Zach. "Parents should be married, don't ya think, Zach?"

Zach said, "Yes, I do think parents should be married. Sometimes, it's not always possible, but it's the right way to do things." His words were glib, but Annie detected the underlying edge to them. "However, I think this conversation is tiring Annie. I'm going to help her upstairs, then the four of us can talk some more about this, if you want."

After hugs from the guys, Annie went to the bedroom with Lily. She dozed, then fed the baby while Zach took the boys home. He returned just after Lily had finished her lunch.

"Thanks for bringing the boys here," Annie told Zach when he came into the bedroom.

He gave her a weak smile.

"And thanks for your comments. It's important for them to know—"

"Shh," he said sincerely. "Let's not get into this. Now's not the time." He lay down opposite her while Lily slept peacefully between them. Smells of baby powder and milk wafted around them.

"She's so tiny." Zach outlined Lily's small fingers with one of his.

"Seven pounds is big for a baby who's four weeks early."

"Yeah, well, she practically fits in my two hands."

Smiling, Annie reached over and ran her knuckles over his jaw. "You need a shave."

"I haven't had time to shower yet today. I'd forgotten how much care a baby demands."

Annie yawned. "How many times were we up last night?"

"Four."

"You didn't have to get up with me every time."

"I wanted to. I'm going to give her a bottle tonight, right, so you can sleep through one of the feedings?"

"Yes. But you sleep through one, too. No sense in us both getting worn-out."

"It's a deal."

Zach stood and stretched, the long lines of his body clothed in a rumpled denim shirt and jeans. Leaning over, he gently took Lily off the bed. She didn't wake as he cuddled her to his chest, then placed her in the bassinet in the corner of the room. Annie was struck again at how experienced he was at caring for an infant. He came back to sit on the bed. "I've got to make a few calls."

"Where?"

"For one, to work."

"How are they doing without you?"

"Fine. Devon's shown a lot of initiative during this whole thing."

"You can go into the office if you want. I can call my mother, or yours."

"No. We both wanted this whole week alone, with no one else staying here." He placed a kiss on her shoulder. "You've already had too many visitors."

"I know. But we couldn't turn our family away."

"Or the boys."

She said, "Les didn't look good last night, did he?"

Zach's shoulders tensed. "No."

"Anything new with the case?"

"Not that I know of." Zach pulled down the bed-covers, then tugged at her arm. "Come on. You don't need to concern yourself with the case right now. You should take a nap while Lily does."

"I have to feed her again in two hours," Annie said, climbing under the blankets.

"Greedy little sucker, isn't she?"

Annie smiled, settling into the pillow. She grasped Zach's hand before he could leave and kissed it. She was still as overcome by her feelings for this man as she'd been since she went into labor. "Will you sleep with me after your shower and calls?"

Leaning over, he brushed her closed eyes with his lips. "I'll sleep with you for the rest of my life, love."

She thought he'd left, but when she heard a rustle,

she opened her eyes. Zach was at the bassinet, staring down at the baby. The profound, tender look on his face affected Annie deeply.

She'd have to think about Sam's comment when she woke up.

AT SIX O'CLOCK the next morning, Annie found Zach stretched out on the couch, Lily clasped to his naked chest. He'd been with the baby the whole night. When Annie wouldn't settle after her 2 o'clock feeding, Zach had gotten up and walked her while Annie slept. He'd never come back to bed. The sight of them now flooded her with love for them both. She sat down in the rocker and watched him.

He'd been a wonder with the baby…

Her navel's fine, Annie, it's supposed to be this red…yes, she's warm enough, but if you swaddle her like this, she can't flail her arms and scare herself… It's okay to give her one bottle a day, it's good for her, actually… You're just tired, honey… That's why you're crying… Get some sleep and I'll listen for her…

To Annie, his expertise was a godsend, though it made her sad because it proved once again how much of a caregiver he'd been to his brothers and sisters. Knowing now what it took to deal with an infant, Zach's childhood seemed even more unfair.

Lily stirred and raised her head. Annie jumped up and went to the couch before the baby could wake Zach.

But it was too late. His hands gripped Lily, making her squall.

"It's all right, I've got her, Zach."

Sleepy-eyed, rumpled, he stared at Annie. His beloved blue eyes were muddy with fatigue. Sinking back down, he buried his face in the pillows.

"Why don't you go upstairs?" she told him. "I'll take over."

"No," he mumbled groggily. "I'm fine."

She smiled. He fell back to sleep in seconds, now that he knew Lily was all right.

Back on the rocker, as Lily suckled noisily, Annie stared at he ex-husband. When had she become convinced she was ready to marry him again?

"When, Lily?" she whispered to the baby. "When Daddy got us through the delivery? When he cried when he saw you? When he walked with you all last night so I could sleep?" A thousand images of Zach whirled through her brain.

Smiling, she raised Lily to burp her. "Shall we tell him when he wakes up, sweetheart?" she whispered to her daughter. "Tell him it's time to make us legally his?"

ZACH WOKE feeling fuzzy and disoriented. He was on the living-room couch, and the December sun filtered through the window. He glanced at the old clock over the fireplace. Noon. Dragging himself off the sofa, he headed up the stairs. At Lily's doorway, he stopped to check on her. They'd put the baby's bassinet in her own room, hoping she might sleep better. Right now, she nestled against the bumper, her pink-flowered fanny in the air, sleeping like an angel.

Yeah, some angel, Zach thought, smiling to himself.

The smile died when he entered Annie's room. She was lying in bed—covered with sweat. Her cheeks were red and her breathing shallow.

Kneeling beside her, he asked, "Sweetheart, what is it?"

She looked at him with too-bright eyes. "I don't know. I don't feel well. It started about ten o'clock."

He touched her forehead. It was alarmingly hot. Without a word, he went to the bathroom and returned with a thermometer.

By then, she was shaking with chills. "Here," he said, sticking the thermometer into her mouth. He held her hand while they waited for the beep.

"What is it?"

"High."

"What?"

"A hundred and three."

Annie's eyes widened.

He said, "I'm calling Kathryn."

It took ten minutes to get through to the midwife. "Give her Tylenol and sponge her down," she told him.

"What's causing this?"

"Ask her if her breasts hurt anywhere."

"Do your breasts hurt?"

Annie nodded.

"Check it, Zach."

Gently, Zach tugged at the delicate buttons on Annie's nursing gown. "There's a big red spot on her left breast," he said into the phone.

"See if it's lumpy."

Annie moaned when he touched it.

"Yes."

"It's probably a clogged milk duct."

He told Annie, "A clogged milk duct." He said to Kathryn, "Is it serious?"

"Not if it's taken care of. Now, here's what you do…"

When Zach hung up the phone, he gave Annie some Tylenol and bathed her in tepid water. It made her shiver. Then he got the heating pad and helped her adjust it over the sore area.

All the while, Annie moaned. "Soon, sweetheart, the Tylenol will take effect soon."

She began to sweat again. Purposefully, he quelled the panic rising inside him. He mopped her forehead and murmured nonsense words to her.

He was going for more water for a second sponge bath, when Lily started to cry. He got the baby and brought her to Annie.

"Here, sweetheart, try to feed her. Kathryn said it will help clear the duct, the more Lily eats."

Annie slid down on the mattress while Zach placed the baby on the bed. Lily nursed vigorously—while

Annie perspired and closed her eyes—to block the pain, he guessed. He swallowed hard, forcing himself to be calm.

When Lily was done, Zach changed her, then put her in the crib.

She screamed.

Picking her up again, he came back to the bedroom. The heating pad had slipped from Annie's breast and Kathryn had said heat was crucial to unclog the duct. Zach sat down, replaced the pad with one hand, holding the baby with the other. As soon as he sat, Lily began to squall again.

Zach looked around, his heart beating fast in his chest.

He had to bathe Annie again.

He had to make sure she kept the heating pad on.

Lily continued to scream.

"Damn," he said.

Spying the phone, he grabbed it to call Sonya. When the machine picked up, he left a brief message, then he hung up and dialed his mother.

"Hello."

Lily drowned out his answer.

"Pa, it's Zach," he repeated. "Is Ma there?"

John snorted. "No, she went to see a psychic with Sonya."

"Oh, hell."

"What's wrong?"

"Annie's sick and Lily's screaming her head off."

He transferred the baby to his other shoulder and patted her back.

"I have to do some things for Annie..."

"I'll be right there."

Forty-five minutes later, Annie's temperature had climbed to a hundred and four. But at least Lily was quiet—somewhere downstairs with his father. Clutching the phone in one hand, Zach kept the heating pad on Annie's breast as he dialed Kathryn again.

"If it reaches a hundred and five you'll have to come to emergency," Kathryn told him. "They'll put Annie on a cooling blanket. Keep close tabs on her temperature."

Swallowing hard, Zach resumed his ministrations.

At three o'clock, her temperature was still a hundred and four.

At four o'clock, it had gone down to a hundred and three again.

She fed Lily, and John Sloan whisked the baby away.

At 6:00 p.m., Annie's fever finally broke.

Zach practically wept with relief. After helping her into a clean nightgown, and changing the sheets, he settled her back to bed. Then he went downstairs.

His father rocked Lily and talked to her. "And someday, I'll take you fishin'. Your daddy loved to fish. You'll like it, too."

Drained, Zach stumbled into the living room and collapsed on the sofa. John held his finger to his mouth, as he got up and brought the baby to the smaller crib situated in the corner of the room. Gently, he placed Lily facedown, then rubbed her back when she stirred.

"You're pretty good at that," Zach said.

"Yeah. I guess it's like riding a bike. You never forget."

He studied his son. "Annie better?"

"Uh-huh. Her fever broke." Zach stared at his father. "I was scared, Pa."

"A man gets scared when he thinks something might happen to the woman he loves."

Suddenly, Martin Mann's leering face flashed before him.

"You take care of Annie real good, son," John said.

How's Annie's car?

The front door opened. "Zach, Annie, it's me," Sonya called from the foyer.

Just in the nick of time. Now that her mother could take care of Annie, Zach had something very important to do. He would wait no longer.

THE CORRIGAN HOUSE was dark when Zach drove up to it. Since the den was in the back, he got out of the car and took the small walkway around to the rear of the property. Sure enough, one dim lamp burned in Les's favorite room.

Zach rang the back doorbell. No one answered. When he tried the knob, it turned easily. A very bright moon helped him find his way to the den doorway.

Les was sitting on his recliner, both hands gripping a bottle of liquor. A fire had burned down, its dying embers adding to the gloom instead of making the room cozy. Les stared at a far wall. Tracking his gaze, Zach saw the memorabilia covering an expanse of about fifteen feet of wall space. Though he couldn't see the individual pieces clearly, he knew there were golf trophies, plaques honoring Les as a civic leader, engineering degrees and framed photos. If he remembered correctly, there was even a shot of him and Les at their college graduation, cocky, arrogant and ready to take on life.

"Hello, Les," Zach said simply.

Les's head came up fast. "What are you doing here?"

"We need to talk."

"Give up on me, Zach."

"Why, because you've given up on yourself?"

Les shook his head.

"Where's Marion?"

"She took Jason. She's staying with her mother for a few days."

"Why?"

"Because she married a loser."

Zach came farther into the room. "Did she?" There was a large leather ottoman in front of the recliner and Zach dropped onto it. He linked his hands between his knees, faced his friend and said,

"I wonder just how much of a loser you really are."
This close, he could see Les clench the open bottle
of Johnny Walker Black. It was half-full. "Why are
you drinking, Les?"

"Because I've lost everything."

"No, you'll lose everything if you keep at the
booze."

"It doesn't matter."

"I think it does."

"You're a good friend, Zach."

"Am I?" When Les didn't answer, he continued,
"Then why have I let you get away with this cha-
rade?"

Les wouldn't meet his eyes. "Don't know what
you're talking about." His voiced was strained.

"Why won't you look at me?"

Still, Les didn't meet Zach's stare.

"Look at me, Les. Look at me when I tell you
that my wife and daughter are in danger because of
Martin Mann."

Les's head snapped up again. His features were
drawn tight with disbelief. "You don't know what
you're talking about."

"No, *you* don't know what you're dealing with."

Drawing back into himself, Les said, "I don't
know what you mean."

"Of course you do. I need facts now, Les. I need
the truth."

"What did you mean about Annie?"

Zach drew in a deep breath. "Mann paid me a

little visit. He hinted that he was having Annie watched. That he could hurt her.''

''No...'' Les bolted off his seat, the scotch falling to the floor with a thunk. Liquor spewed onto the rug, stinging Zach's nostrils.

Les began to pace. ''No, it's not supposed to happen like this. He told me...he told me no one would get hurt this way...he said—'' Les stopped talking abruptly and whirled to Zach.

Zach stood, too. ''He said what, Les? Tell me exactly how Mann talked you into taking the fall for the collapse of the staircase.''

''He didn't talk me into anything. I'm guilty, Zach. It's as simple as that.''

''What are you guilty of, Les? And don't try to convince me you've told the whole story. I don't believe it.''

Stubbornly Les remained silent. Zach crossed to him and grabbed his arm. ''I don't want you to be blamed for the staircase's collapse if it isn't all your fault. I love you like a brother. But if you won't tell the whole truth for yourself, you've got to do it for Annie. Because I'll never let you jeopardize her for some false sense of responsibility. I won't let it go, Les. Do you hear me? I won't.'' He took a step back and crossed his arms over his chest. ''So you might as well tell me now.''

Right before Zach's eyes, Les crumbled. His shoulders sagged and tears began to stream down his cheeks. He sank onto a straight chair by the wall and covered his face with his hands. "I had no idea the plan would go like this."

Zach knelt before his friend. "Tell me, Les."

After long seconds, Les uncovered his face. His eyes met Zach's. "The day the pits were dug…I had a hangover, like I said. Marion and I had had a terrible fight the night before, and I turned to the booze. All that was the truth."

"Okay."

"Because I wasn't used to the liquor anymore, I was sick that morning. I wanted to go home and sleep. By noon, we dug eight pits, and the results were the same. Gravelly soil. No clay. No pockets."

"Go on."

"Mann cornered me—asked me what was wrong with me."

Zach's heart sped up. "Mann was there."

"Yes. He was supposed to have dental surgery, but it was delayed a day."

Zach heard Jonathan Gumby's words, *I'm gonna check out one more thing. The doctor was out of town right up until that day. I wanna check the flights and stuff—that's where I was going when the accident happened.*

"Anyway," Les continued, "I told Martin I felt sick. He told me to go home. He'd supervise the rest of the pits."

"I see. Did you go home?"

"Yeah, I signed off on the log for the eight pits

I'd supervised." He held Zach's gaze as he confessed, "And then I signed for the last four."

"The ones that weren't dug yet."

"Yes." Les grabbed his arm. "But the soil condition was adequate for the first eight. Chances were, the soil would be adequate for the rest of the pits, too." Les swore, then said, "Mann promised me he'd call me if anything came up with the other four pits. He promised me, Zach."

"But he didn't."

"No."

Zach got up, grabbed a chair by the desk, brought it around and straddled it, facing his friend.

"What happened, really?"

"They found an old mine shaft when they were on the last pit. Martin contended it was still a judgment call, whether or not the soil needed fill, but he was lying. Of course, I didn't know that at the time."

"You know that now? For sure?"

"Yeah. When the staircase fell, the original shovel operator panicked and called me. He told me it was pretty clear-cut the pit needed fill."

Zach sighed. "Les, I still don't understand why you took the blame."

"Because I'm at fault."

"For signing logs prematurely. Not for causing the staircase to fall."

"I would have lost my license anyway."

"Probably."

Les said nothing else.

"How did Mann convince you to do this, to take the full blame?"

"He said that we'd both go down, if everything came out. And that if I took the blame alone, said it was a judgment call on my part, I'd only lose my license, like I was going to anyway."

"Ah, I get it. And if the whole truth came out—Mann had knowingly concealed a subsoil condition to save money—then he could be charged with criminal negligence."

"Yes. Since I had nothing to gain by concealing the condition—the standard contract said that Mann assumed all costs of preparing the ground—the authorities would believe that it *was* really a judgment call."

"And either way, you'd lose your license."

"Yes. Mann said he'd find work for me, if I cooperated. That there were plenty of jobs in contracting that I could get without an engineer's license. He'd take care of me."

Zach stood and paced the length of the den. "You still made a bad choice, Les."

"Zach, I had no idea you or Annie could be hurt by my confession. I thought it would exonerate you."

"Did he threaten you in any way?"

"Only indirectly." Les stood, too, stuffing his hands in his pockets. "He said if word got out about my drinking, then even subcontractors wouldn't hire me."

"So you went along with it."

"It seemed the best route." Les hesitated, then said, "And he's paying for my lawyer."

Zach stopped and stared at Les. "Not anymore, buddy." Determined, he strode to the phone on the desk, picked it up and dialed. After three rings, Spence Campbell answered. "Spence, I want to see you tonight. I have somebody who needs your help."

After he hung up, Zach crossed to Les. Without another word, he reached out and hugged his friend.

CHAPTER FOURTEEN

ANNIE LAY on the bed watching the light streaming through the window make crisscross patterns on Zach's back as he slept. Though most of yesterday was a blur because of her illness, she knew he'd taken care of her through the worst of it, then he'd gone out. Her mother had stayed with her and Lily until Zach had returned around three in the morning. He'd fed the baby, while Annie had fallen back into a deep sleep. When she awoke for Lily's six o'clock feeding, Zach was out cold beside her.

He stirred, burrowing his face into the pillow. Eyes still closed, he reached for her, as he did every morning they awoke together. She'd forgotten how sexy it all was. He was naked, the sheet draped loosely at his hips. Spanning her waist with his hand, he inched closer, tugging her toward him at the same time. He nudged his face in her nightgowned breasts and breathed in.

"Mmm...you smell good."

Slowly, languishing in the man she loved, she stroked his mussed hair. "I've had a shower."

"What time is it?"

"Almost seven."

He opened one eye. "Lily?"

"Fed, changed and back asleep."

Rising onto his elbows, he said, "You okay? I just remembered…"

"All better." She leaned over and kissed his cheek. It was scratchy. "You took good care of me."

Smiling, he snuggled back into the pillow.

"Want more sleep, or coffee?"

"Coffee."

Perfect, she thought. *Just perfect.* She slid off the bed. After a quick detour to her dresser to get a small velvet pouch, she went downstairs, fixed coffee and a muffin, put it on a tray and came back upstairs. After placing the food and drink on the night table, she dropped onto the edge of the mattress.

Zach rolled over, sat up, scrubbed his hands down his face and propped himself against the headboard. His eyes still closed, he sipped the coffee she'd handed him. After a few minutes, he yawned and opened his eyes. Then he leaned over and kissed her.

"Mmm…better than the coffee."

She buried her face in his neck. He smelled like sleep and musk.

Coming fully awake, he pulled back and frowned. "Annie, we've got to talk. I've got to—"

"Not yet. I want to tell you something first."

Sleepy eyes stared out at her, accompanied by a rakish grin. "Mine's better."

Linking her hand with his free one, she smiled. "It couldn't be. I want you to know I've decided that it doesn't matter what you do or don't do about Les's involvement in the building's collapse. I've been terribly wrong to push you to do anything. I'm letting go of that concern, and anything else that keeps us apart.''

She didn't understand when he threw back his head and laughed. ''Zach?''

Shaking his head, he looked at her, his eyes brimming with love. ''This is so typical of us. I've got something to tell you.''

''It won't matter. Nothing will change how I feel…ever again,'' she promised solemnly. ''I—'' The phone rang, interrupting what Annie wanted to say. ''Let the machine pick it up.''

Zach was already reaching over her for the phone. ''Can't.'' He snatched up the receiver. ''Sloan… Hi, Spence. I thought it might be you… Sure, I can come down.'' He glanced at Annie. ''Give me forty-five minutes, then I'll be there.''

Disgruntled at the interruption of her plans, Annie asked when he hung up, ''Where are you going?''

''To OSHA.'' He rubbed his knuckles on her cheek. ''It's about what I wanted to tell you.''

Annie's heart started beating faster.

''You were right,'' Zach said. ''Les wasn't telling the whole truth about the building.''

''Oh, Zach, I didn't want to be right. I just wanted to help Les.'' Her eyes narrowed on him. ''How do you know all this?''

''I went to see him last night. To get to the bottom

of this mess once and for all.'' Briefly he told her about his conversation with Jonathan Gumby the night Lily was born.

''Why did you decide to do something last night?''

''You're not going to like this,'' he said. ''I've kept some things from you. Martin Mann cornered me in the firm's parking lot the night before Thanksgiving.'' Zach hesitated. ''Annie, he threatened us.''

''*What?*''

Again, he filled her in on the details. Then he grasped her shoulders. ''I was going to tell you, honey, but you went into labor.'' His eyes were alert now, and worried. About her reaction.

''Oh, Zach, I understand why you kept this from me. I could never have handled a threat when I was ready to give birth.''

''You're not mad I didn't tell you?''

She smiled. ''No, I told you I trusted you to do the right thing.''

He breathed out a heavy sigh. ''Yesterday, after you got sick, something clicked with me. I knew I had to resolve this issue right away. So I went to see Les at about seven.''

''What exactly did he confess to?''

''Signing off on the last four test pits before they were dug. He went home sick that day with a hangover. But he signed the logs, trusting Martin Mann to be aboveboard in his findings.''

''Oh, no.''

"Instead, Mann falsified the soil suitability of the last four pits."

"Oh, my God. And a woman died."

"Yes."

She grabbed Zach's hands. They were cold and clammy. "I'm sorry, Zach. You would have been at the site during the digging if we hadn't been in the midst of a divorce."

Raking a hand through his hair, he said, "I'm so tired of these recriminations. I want it all to be over."

And I want it all to begin again, Annie thought. "Zach, before you go—" A squall came from Lily's room. "Damn."

Zach chuckled. "You'd better go get her while I shower. We'll talk later."

"Wait. Just one thing," she said, halting him with a hand on his bare shoulder. "I'm so proud of you. You're a wonderful man, a terrific father and a great friend. I love you." *And I'm never letting you go again,* she thought but didn't say aloud. Instead, she rose and went to take care of Zach's baby.

HARD HATS IN PLACE, Zach and Les Corrigan walked around the inside of the Pierce Museum a week later with Tom Watson.

"I think it can be done," Les said, his voice strong, though his face was drawn and his eyes sad. "Since the building was constructed on a hill, we can probably go back in through the ground, shore up the soil and reposition the beams. The staircase can be braced in other ways, too. Don't you think so, Zach?''

Slowly, Zach scanned the interior of the museum's main room. It had been cleaned up, and the upper-floor staircase braced. But the ravages of the collapse were glaringly evident in the broken glass and boards and the cracked plaster. As with people, wounds healed but they left scars. "Yeah. I definitely think it can be made safe again." Things *can* be fixed, he told himself. "We should consult some experts, though. And we might want to get in touch with builders and architects in other cities where parts of buildings have caved in. I know the designer of the hotel in San Francisco where the walkway collapsed a few years ago. They rebuilt it. I'll call him today."

"Good," Watson said. "We appreciate the help. Especially yours," he said pointedly to Corrigan. "With all you're going through."

Les's eyes were bleak. "It's the least I can do."

Watson nodded. "Well, I'm meeting with the owners in the other wing at ten o'clock. Take care," he said and left.

When Watson had gone, Zach said, "You okay, buddy?"

Corrigan nodded. "I'll be all right."

"Want to talk?"

Les trudged over and stared out the row of windows in the back of the museum's first floor. "Yeah, I guess." He ran a hand through his hair and was silent for a while.

After a moment, Zach followed him. "Spence said you've gone back to AA."

"I never should have left. Spence thought it would look good for the hearing next week if I'd taken some steps to show I've changed, but I would have done it anyway. I need to take control of my life."

"What about Marion? Have you seen her since Mann's arraignment?"

Les sighed. "No."

It had been a week since Les had confessed the real circumstances of the test pits. In a whirlwind of activity, Mann had been indicted on the charge of criminal negligence—and was facing charges for causing Jonathan Gumby's accident. Les had been cleared of criminal action but had lost his engineering license, and was facing an uncertain future professionally. The Barton family lawsuit was still pending. Les was trying to pick up the pieces of his life, and Zach spent time with him, to help as much as he could. Consequently, Zach had seen too little of Annie and his almost-two-week-old daughter.

"What's on for today?" Zach asked glancing at his watch.

"That's the tough part." Les's hands were shaking as he stuck them in his pockets. "Not having anything to do all day. I get to see Jason tonight, though."

Zach smiled. "Why don't you bring him over to visit with the baby. He loved it the last time—"

Both Zach and Les turned when the front door to

the museum opened. Framed in the entryway was Annie.

And Marion Corrigan.

"Hello, guys," Annie said cheerfully. "Want some company?"

Zach bit his lip to keep from scolding her for being out too soon after Lily's birth. Kathryn had said she shouldn't drive for at least two weeks.

"Marion." Les's gravelly voice drew Zach away from his concern about Annie.

Marion left the doorway and crossed the floor, skirting the amputated staircase. Zach saw Annie staring at the broken glass and oak solemnly, myriad emotions crossing her face.

Les's wife stood in front of him. "You look tired, Les," she said, reaching up and laying her hand on his cheek. "I…" She cleared her throat. "I've come to take you home."

Tears sparkled in Les's eyes, caught in the mid-December-morning sunlight that reflected off the snow outside. "Home? With you?"

Marion nodded. "We miss you. We need you." With a heavy sigh, she looked around the museum. "This place has run our lives long enough. Let's get out of here."

Deeply moved, Zach turned away as Les drew his wife into a solid embrace. Crossing to Annie, Zach smiled as he got closer. She had on a light winter jacket; beneath it she was dressed in maternity jeans and an oversize "Mom" sweatshirt. She wore no makeup and her hair was pulled back from her face with clips. She looked absolutely beautiful.

Zach said, "Hello, love. How are you?"

"Hi, hotshot. I feel great today."

"What are you doing here?" Though he tried not to, he added, "You shouldn't be out of the house yet."

She scowled, but it had no punch. "Still bossing me around?"

He ran his hand down her hair. "Yeah, I am."

She chuckled. "Well, I figured if I wanted some time alone with you, I'd better get out of that house. Between my mother and your parents, it's a zoo. When Marion came to visit today, I suggested a drive."

He hooked an arm around her neck, pulling her close. "Who's with the holy terror?"

Annie rolled her eyes at the apt description of the child who now ran their household. "Grandpa. She seems to behave best with him."

Zach smiled at the image of his father rocking Lily and talking to her. "Did you suggest this, too?" he asked, angling his head to the Corrigans.

"No. When Marion saw an article about the museum in the morning paper, she told me she wanted to talk to Les. I said I happened to know where he was right then."

"You're a good friend, Annie."

She reached up and kissed Zach's cheek. "So are you."

"Well, we're leaving," Marion said from behind them.

Annie turned to see the Corrigans, framed by the shattered staircase, holding hands. Hugging Les first, then her friend, she whispered to the other woman, "I'll call you when we decide."

"You'd better."

Zach and Les said goodbye and hugged warmly. When they'd gone, Zach tugged Annie to him. "Let's get out of here, too. You don't have a hard hat on."

She was staring over his shoulder at the staircase, then her eyes scanned the whole museum. "Wait a minute. I came here for a specific reason, too."

Zach's eyes took on a familiar glow. "Well, if it's for any hanky-panky, let me remind you the doctor said six weeks."

"Hey, there are other ways…"

"And the OSHA officials are back in the museum offices." Zach cocked his head toward the west wing.

"Oh, damn, well then I guess I'll just have to settle for this." She drew a small velvet pouch out of her pocket and placed it in his hand. "I've wanted to give you this since the morning after Les told the truth. But things have been so crazy, there just wasn't the right time." Again she scanned the museum. "Besides, I think this is the appropriate place to do it. This museum—what it represented—tore us apart. Then it brought you back to me."

Zach's eyes shimmered with the sadness and the hope her words reflected. He fondled the bag. "What is it?"

"Open it and see."

His big fingers tugged on the drawstring. It was too small to get his hand inside, so he shook out the contents into his palm—and froze.

She saw his Adam's apple work vigorously. His lashes lowered and his left hand fisted briefly.

Reverently, he grasped the small gold ring and circled it with his index finger. When he looked up at her, his eyes were hazy with hurt. "You said you destroyed this. You told me," he said hoarsely, "that you threw it out…"

"I didn't Zach, I couldn't."

Lifting it, he ran his fingertip along the inside, over the sentimental inscription: I.L.Y.M.T.A.E.I.T.W. *I Love You More Than Anything Else In The World* He coughed to clear his throat but didn't say anything. Deliberately she raised her left hand and held it out. He swallowed hard again, locked his eyes with hers and slid the ring on her finger. Just as it had the first time, it stopped at her knuckle; he gently shoved it over. Then, as he'd done almost fifteen years before, he brought her hand with his wedding ring on it to his lips.

She rose on tiptoe and kissed his cheek. Then she took the bag from him and shook out what he'd missed. Zach gasped when he saw his own wedding band in her palm. "Oh, Annie," he said, letting out a ragged breath. "I'd left it on the dresser that morning. You kept it, too...I can't believe...I..." He shook his head.

Moved by the strength of his emotion, Annie's hand trembled. Reaching down, she took his left hand and replaced the band on his finger. Then her eyes clouded. It looked right.

"I want to marry you again, Zachary Sloan," she said earnestly. "Right away."

Gently he pulled her to him, nestling her head in his shoulder. "I thought I'd never hear you say that." The hurt in his voice tugged at her heart.

She cuddled into him. "I know. I'm sorry it took so long." Peering up into his deep blue eyes, she said, "But I'm never letting you go again. So what do you say?"

"I say yes," he murmured against her mouth. "Yes. Yes. *Yes.*"

EPILOGUE

TWO-YEAR-OLD Lily Anne Sloan tore out of her mother's grasp and ran into the arms of Nora Farnum, the receptionist-turned-administrative assistant for the newly incorporated Sloan and McCade Associates. Annie pressed her hand into her stomach as she watched the little girl—who looked exactly like her father with dark blond hair and blue eyes that could melt steel—race to greet the older woman.

"Hi, Lily," Nora said, "Daddy's waiting for you."

"Daddy…Daddy…Daddy," Lily chanted as she reached for the pencils on Nora's desk.

Scooping her up and away from them, Nora glanced at Annie.

The assistant eyed Annie's denim jumper and loose hair, and probably very pale face. "Are you all right, Annie?"

"Just fine," Annie lied. "Is Zach ready?"

"Almost. He's in a meeting with Les Corrigan, but he said for you to come back when you got here."

Slowly Annie made her way to Zach's office, Lily in tow. The little girl slid her almost-clean hands along the wallpaper and turned a few cartwheels on the plush carpet, but Annie refrained from chastising her mischievous daughter. She just didn't have the energy.

Lily swung open the door to her father's chic office and barreled in. Zach pushed out from behind his desk in time to catch her from a running leap.

"Hi, sweetheart," he said, smoothing down her long curly locks.

"Hi, Daddy."

Sticking her finger in her mouth, she cuddled into his red T-shirt, which matched hers, plopped her sneakers on his jeans and turned to look at the other man. When she saw Les, she skittered off her dad's lap and threw herself at him, saying, "Unca Les!"

Les grabbed her at the waist, stood up and threw her into the air. The motion caught Annie unaware—and her hand flew to her stomach. "Excuse me," she said and raced to the bathroom.

His eyes narrowed, Zach watched Annie go.

"Something wrong?" Les asked.

Zach's grin was followed by a chuckle. "Nope, I think everything is just perfect. Watch the squirt, will you? I'll be right back."

He found Annie standing over the toilet. He crossed to her and smoothed back the hair from her chalk-white face. Sliding one hand around her back and another under her knees, he picked her up and carried her to the chair in the corner of the bathroom.

He sat down, nestled her face in the crook of his neck and put a hand over her womb. "When?"

"Christmastime, again."

He closed his eyes to savor the pure joy surging through him. Then he drew back. "Honey, I hope you were really ready. I know I've been pushing you…"

Annie snuggled into him. "Pushing me? You've been a bulldozer."

"I have."

"I wanted him, too."

"Him?"

She looked up at Zach with the smile that still turned him to mush and could make him promise her the moon. "Yes. I think I'll have a boy this time. You can name him."

After a pause, Zach said, "How about John Zachary Sloan?"

"Hmm…nice."

Caressing her tummy, Zach said, "Hi, buddy." His voice was hoarse, his hand not quite steady. "This is your daddy."

Annie sighed and shifted closer to him. They held each other in contented silence.

"You still want to come to the game?" Zach asked, trying hard to stifle the concern in his voice. "I can take Lily and you can go home and rest."

"Are you kidding?" She tugged at Zach's team shirt. "This is the City Slickers' opening game. Besides, Les and his family will be there, won't they?"

"Marion can't make it. The boutique is having their annual summer sale. Her co-worker got sick."

"Oh. Well, we'll get to see Jason, though, won't we? Lily's been asking about him all day."

"Yeah. Les is picking him up right after he drops off the new sketches for Gage's warehouse."

"Who would have thought Jackson would take such a liking to Les after all that happened? Les is happy working in business, isn't he?"

"He's happy being sober, with his marriage on the upswing. They're talking about having another baby, too. His professional life takes second fiddle to everything else now." Zach peered down at Annie, threading his hand through her hair. "Not like someone else I know."

"Don't bully me, Zach."

He reached out to touch her stomach again. "Are you kidding? I'm going to bully you for nine whole months. I'm really proud of the fact that you're now a Ph.D., but you'll have to take some time off from your private practice to get through these first few weeks, Annie. Remember the last pregnancy."

Closing her eyes, she said, "Oh, God, don't remind me."

"Have you thought about hiring a partner?"

"Zach, just because it clicked for you and Devon…"

"It's how I can work only three days a week."

And donate one of those days off to the Inner City

Housing Project. She stared at him, then sighed. "Actually, I started interviewing today."

"I knew you'd do the right thing." He nuzzled her neck with his nose. "I'll stop badgering you now."

"When hell freezes over," she mumbled into his shirt.

"What was that, little girl?"

"Nothing, hotshot. Just shut up and kiss me."

He lowered his head and took her mouth gently at first. Then the kiss turned deep, and long and luscious.

"Annie…"

"Zach…" She breathed the word into his ear, her arms encircling his neck, her body molding to his.

He put her away from him. "We'd better go tell our daughter about her brother," he said huskily, "before I forget she's out there in the next room." He stood abruptly and set Annie on her feet.

She blanched with the sudden change of position.

"Sorry."

"Will you stop and get me a milk shake before the game?"

"I'll do anything you ask," he said, his voice full with emotion. "I love you, Annie."

She laced her hands with his. Her wedding band pressed against his finger and he felt his dig into the base of his hand.

Annie said, "I love you, too, Zach. More than anything else in the world."

SILHOUETTE® SUPERROMANCE™

AVAILABLE FROM 18TH OCTOBER 2002

JUST AROUND THE CORNER
Tara Taylor Quinn

Shelter Valley

Phyllis Langford is everybody's friend and nobody's lover—
until she succumbs to the temptation of loner Matt
Sheffield! Soon after, she discovers she's pregnant. She
wants nothing from Matt—but Matt can't leave it like that…

ACCIDENTALLY YOURS Rebecca Winters

FBI agent Max Calder is working undercover to bring down
a Russian Mafia ring. He infiltrates the group, but Gaby
Peris, an attractive widow, somehow ends up in the middle
of the action. Is she an innocent victim or part of the scam?
Max *has* to find out—because he's starting to fall for her…

LAST-MINUTE MARRIAGE Marisa Carroll

Riverbend

Single father Mitch Sterling has a lot on his plate. His
shop is competing with a national chain and he's taking
care of his grandfather as well as his son. Then he meets a
pregnant, stranded, single woman who needs a friend.
And if Mitch is honest, he'll admit that he wants to be
more than her friend…

BABY BUSINESS Brenda Novak

Nine Months Later

Macy McKinney will do *anything* to find money for her
five-year-old daughter's operation. So when businessman
Thad Winters wants a child without the complications of a
relationship, he hires Macy to have his baby! Once Macy
is pregnant they decide that a temporary marriage will
simplify the situation—but will it?

DELIVERED BY

Christmas

Linda Howard
Joan Hohl   Sandra Steffen

Available from 18th October 2002

1102/128/SH41

▼™ SILHOUETTE®
SUPERROMANCE™
Welcomes you to

RIVERBEND

Riverbend… the kind of place where everyone knows your name — and your business. Riverbend… home of a group of small-town sons and daughters who've been friends since school.

They're all grown up now. Living their lives and learning that you can get through anything as long as you have your friends.

Five wonderful stories:

0802/SH/LC37

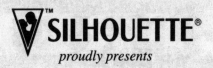

SILHOUETTE®

proudly presents

five wonderful, warm stories from bestselling author

SHERRYL WOODS

The Calamity Janes

Five unique women share a lifetime of friendship!

DO YOU TAKE THIS REBEL?

Silhouette Special Edition
October 2002

COURTING THE ENEMY

Silhouette Special Edition
November 2002

TO CATCH A THIEF

Silhouette Special Edition
December 2002

THE CALAMITY JANES

Silhouette Superromance
January 2003

WRANGLING THE REDHEAD

Silhouette Special Edition
February 2003

1002/SH/LC42

2 FREE

books and a surprise gift!

We would like to take this opportunity to thank you for reading this Silhouette® book by offering you the chance to take TWO more specially selected titles from the Superromance™ series absolutely FREE! We're also making this offer to introduce you to the benefits of the Reader Service™—

- ★ FREE home delivery
- ★ FREE gifts and competitions
- ★ FREE monthly Newsletter
- ★ Exclusive Reader Service discount
- ★ Books available before they're in the shops

Accepting these FREE books and gift places you under no obligation to buy, you may cancel at any time, even after receiving your free shipment. Simply complete your details below and return the entire page to the address below. *You don't even need a stamp!*

YES! Please send me 2 free Superromance books and a surprise gift. I understand that unless you hear from me, I will receive 4 superb new titles every month for just £3.49 each, postage and packing free. I am under no obligation to purchase any books and may cancel my subscription at any time. The free books and gift will be mine to keep in any case.

U2ZEA

Ms/Mrs/Miss/Mr ....Initials...............................
BLOCK CAPITALS PLEASE

Surname ....

Address ....

....

....Postcode..............................

Send this whole page to:
UK: FREEPOST CN81, Croydon, CR9 3WZ
EIRE: PO Box 4546, Kilcock, County Kildare (stamp required)